WOLF MOON

THE GRAZI KELLY NOVEL SERIES 1

C.D. GORRI

COPYRIGHT

BLURB

"Hi. My name is Grazi Kelly. There are things I know are true and things that I never would have guessed. First, demons and witches exist and they are evil. Second, the world is up for grabs and the witches are getting their minions ready. Third, I'm a werewolf and it's my job to stop them."

High school sophomore Grazi Kelly leads an ordinary life in the suburbs of New Jersey helping her grandmother with chores and attending Catholic school. Things are pretty good except for her bullying cousin and the rest of the obnoxious cheer team.

Things take a frightening turn when the night of the full moon arrives and the bodies start piling up. Grazi learns that she is different in ways she never expected.

Torn between Sebastian, the school soccer star and Ronan, a foreign exchange student who shares her secret. She must uncover the identity behind the mysterious attacker, but is she ready for the entire truth?

DEDICATION

To my family, thank you for your continued support and unconditional love. You gave me the courage to give Grazi her voice. You are my eternal inspiration. All my love, xoxo.

Special thanks to Tammy Payne from Book Nook Nuts for editing this version! You rock!

1

"Mama, tell me again. Please, Mama, tell me, tell me, tell meeee!" My voice sounded childish even to my ears. I must have been only two or three. I could almost make out my mother's face, but it remained infuriatingly blurry. I snuggled down in my tiny bed with its pink and white quilt. My favorite rubber ducky was on the pillow next to my head, and I held my little hand sewn rag doll tightly in my chubby little hands. I loved that house. My room was pink and white, and there was always a mess of toys scattered across the floor, but Mama never seemed to mind. She and Daddy would get down on the floor with me and play princesses anytime I wanted.

"Okay, okay. Ti amo, Maria bella, ti amo del mare

alla stella!" Her soft chestnut hair tickled my face as she bent to tuck me in. I giggled. My mother smiled and kissed me several times on my cheek. I could feel her. I clutched at her with my tiny hands and breathed her in. I loved her smell, baby powder and Ivory soap and just Mama. She took my hands gently from around her neck and kissed both of them before placing them on the blanket.

"Tell me what it means, mama! Tell me, tell me! Pleeease!"

"I will, I will. Hush now, my baby." She tucked in the blanket all around me and placed the statue of Mary on my nightstand, "Okay, now. You all snug, good! It means I love you, my beautiful Maria, from the sea all the way up to the stars!"

"I love you too, mama! Up to the stars!"

"I know, baby, I know. I love you so much! Now you must promise me that you'll run when I tell you, Maria! Run, Maria! Run! Run! RUN!"

Cold sweat clung to me as I sprang up in my bed. My hands tangled in my long loose hair as I struggled to turn on my bedside lamp. This was a recurring dream or nightmare or both. I guess it depends on how I'm feeling. Sometimes I was so grateful for it, and other times I'd just be so frustrated I couldn't fall back asleep. I never understood why I couldn't see her face. I mean I had photos of her, I know what she looked like, but in my dream, I never saw my mother's face. But her voice, that I heard perfectly. I could hear her as clearly as if she was in the room. Her voice yelling for me to run would sometimes ring in my ears for hours. Weird, but not the weirdest thing to happen to me. I guess I should introduce myself.

My name is Maria Graziana Kelly. People call me Grazi (grah-tzee). I am trying to make sense of everything that has happened to me over the last few months. How I became the person, I am now. A good story has a great beginning. Something that draws you in. Well, I am not trying to impress anyone. Nor am I drawing anyone into some sort of fictional world. This is *real*. I guess you could consider my tale a warning. There are things out there. Things you and I never dreamed existed.

At a time like this, I always go with the classics. *"There are more things in heaven and earth, Horatio than are dreamt of in your philosophy."* That's my absolute favorite Shakespeare quote. Good old Hamlet. Of course, the first time I read it I had no idea how right he was. There was a time I could lose myself in a good play or book and forget the world. Escape from all my so-called problems. You know what I mean. Family, high school, my social life or lack thereof. I should start at the beginning. Give you a little background info.

Both of my parents are dead. My cousin is right when she calls me an orphan. Technically I am one. Mom and dad both died when I was three. I don't remember much about them, but I try. My recurring dream about my mother started when I was about nine. It used to happen only once in a while, but it picked up in frequency as I got older. I live in a suburb in northern New Jersey with my grandmother, Nonna Rosa. It was just us for a few years. Then about eight years ago my Uncle Vito and his family came to live with us when they lost their house down the shore due to a freak hurricane. It was supposed to be temporary, but here we all are. We share a renovated Victorian house on a cul de sac. Vinyl siding, huge yard, white privacy fence, the works.

Nonna Rosa is my maternal grandmother. I never met any of my dad's family. I know he was Irish, that's about it. Anyway, she came to the U.S. from a small town in Southern Italy when she was just a kid. She's a devout Roman Catholic and has taken great pains to educate her family in the tradition of her faith. I have been in Catholic school since pre-k. The same school my mother and uncle both attended. We go to Mass every Sunday, holidays, and all of the Holy days. Our parish priest, Fr. Verrell, is a frequent presence in our house. He and Nonna often play checkers or cards. He comes to most of our holiday dinners. Not that I blame him, my grandmother can seriously cook.

We keep Climbing Clouds in our front yard. They're these tiny white roses that burst out all over, *like clouds*. The bushes surround this three-foot-high, blue and white plaster statue of the Holy Virgin Mary. My grandmother loves those roses. We keep the shrubs immaculately trimmed and weeded. There is another statue of Mary in our back-yard garden. That's where Nonna grows rows and rows of organic vegetables, fruits, and herbs. Every spring Julianna and I, *mostly I*, weed and till the dark soil until Nonna tells us it is ready for planting. And every fall we bring in our modest harvest. It was almost harvest time, and there I was working away another Saturday morning.

"You can finish this, I am so outta here," Julianna threw down the rake and her gardening gloves on one of the benches we had set up in the yard. She stormed off without another glance. She hated yard work and gardening. She always complained about having to do the same chores as me. She's a year older than I am, a junior to my sophomore. The only thing she likes about the Catholic high school we attend is that it happens to be co-ed. Her father told her he was going to send her to an all- girl Academy when she graduated from grammar school, and she had a fit.

I picked up her stuff and put it back in the storage shed. At least now I'd have some peace while I worked. Even though I am technically a sophomore, I placed out of American Literature and Algebra II, so I take both classes with the juniors. That means I get the joy of her company for most of my classes at school too. Sr. Diane, our principal, said if I tried hard enough I might be able to graduate early, but I'm not sure I want to. Julianna hates that too. She either ignores me or knocks my books down when we have class together. I try and sit in the back, keep my head down, but it doesn't matter. The teachers call on me, and I answer. I don't see the point in not answering or trying to get it wrong. Some things just come easily to me.

English Lit is my favorite class. Mrs. Theodore, my teacher, is a middle-aged woman with cat-eyed glasses like you see in fifties movies. She has short brown hair and wears a different color sweater set every day with a long khaki skirt underneath. "Pop quiz," are her favorite words. A chorus of groans usually follows. I don't mind, but then again, I am probably the only student who ever finishes the required reading. Anyway, pop quizzes never bothered me though I admit that teachers get pretty creepy when they announce them. One side of Mrs. Theodore's mouth, which was usually coated in an unflattering shade of orange lipstick, tended to curve up into a mockery of a smile whenever she uttered those words. It was enough to send any student of hers running down the hall and screaming for help. Not that any resorted to that, just average looks of horror and disgust.

That very first week of my sophomore year we had a pop quiz in English Lit. I looked at my sheet of loose leaf to avoid meeting anyone's eyes and wrote a five-paragraph essay comparing and contrasting the Bronte sisters. Our summer reading had been <u>Wuthering Heights</u> and <u>Jane Eyre</u>. I will cop to totally loving them both. In fact, I had finished both books before the second week of summer. I completed the quiz in all of fifteen minutes. Mrs. Theodore let me go early with a pointed glare after grilling me on the benefits of taking one's time when preparing a writing assignment. I waited for her to finish then left class and walked down the empty corridor straight to study hall. An hour later I saw Julianna at lunch. She knocked my tray over. An accident of course. Soggy pizza and milk are a pretty sorry excuse for lunch anyway. That was about as bad as one of my days could get. But that was when things were ordinary. When *I* was ordinary.

It's hard to pinpoint the exact moment when my

life changed. But looking back on it, I would have to say it all started that Saturday in the backyard. Julianna had stormed off about ten minutes after starting, and I was weeding the herb garden. The sun was beating down on my shoulders, and I wished for the hundredth time I had worn a tank top that morning instead of a black t-shirt. It was, after all, September and should have been cooler. But this was one of the driest, hottest summers we had ever had. Nonna called it an "Indian summer". Not politically correct, I know, but according to Google, it was an apt description. Every time I turned on the TV, local anchors reported on the drought and how it was affecting the entire Garden State. The price of eggplant and blueberries around the world had already skyrocketed. Nonna's prize winning tomatoes were shriveled and hard this year and I, I couldn't tell the weeds from the herbs. Everything was brittle and the same shade of pale yellowish green. Not the vibrant dark leaves I was used to. I did my best but didn't feel like I was accomplishing much.

"Maria, come have some iced tea, *cara*," Nonna called from the large wrap around porch my Uncle Vito had built himself. Seven years old and it still looked as if he had just finished laying the wood. I know this because every year I helped clean it with a power washer, sand it down, and slather it with a natural stain in the few weekends of sunshine we had after Easter and before Memorial Day. Every year I worked by my uncle's side and listened to him grumble about the blood and sweat he put into the thing just to make his wife happy. And you guessed it, she never even sat out there. Aunt Theresa was *never* happy. At least never when I was around.

I was grateful for the respite and ambled over. I took my gardening gloves off before I extended my hand to take the cool glass from Nonna's wrinkled old one. Such strength she had in such a delicate looking hand. I've seen her weed, plant, clean, cook, sew, heal, nurture, and pray with those hands. She smiled at me and brushed my damp hair from my forehead. I drank the sweetened tea with its delicate hint of our home-grown mint and fresh lemon juice.

"Where is your cousin? She helped already, *si*?"

"Sure, Nonna, Julianna helped before she went to cheering," I spoke the fib with practiced ease. I usually tried to avoid confrontations and if it meant a white lie here or there to spare my grandmother then fine. Lying never sat very well with me, but confrontations were worse, and I didn't want to fight with my cousin over some weeding.

"No, my girl, she left you to do it alone again, huh?

My poor girl, always the good one. Well, that is that. Anything we could salvage *nel giardino*?" She nodded towards the herbs, and I didn't have the heart to tell her we'd never get a decent harvest this year.

"Maybe, Nonna. Let's wait and see if it rains this weekend."

"We can put the hose on at night. Mrs. Kelly can mind her own business, you know!"

I hid a smile and kissed Nonna on her head. Her mostly white hair was cut short, and the springy curls brushed my cheek. I love my grandmother with all my heart. She became both mother and father to me when I lost my own parents. I love her Italian accent and the way she said my name, *mah-rree-ah*. She made it sound pretty. I love her food! She had to be the best cook around. Especially her Sunday sauce and homemade manicotti. I love the way she yelled out all the wrong answers while watching Jeopardy and the way she sang off-key while she cooked. It is important for you to know this because defying her was something I never thought possible.

I mean I would do anything for her, but she was right. Mrs. Kelly, *no relation*, would report us to the neighborhood watch if we put on our sprinkling system or even our small gardening hose. We were in a drought and were not allowed to use our water for anything other than the necessities. Washing the car, watering the lawn or garden, even filling pools were prohibited during a drought.

I glanced at our yard and over the fence at our neighbor's yard. It was sad really. Lawns that were once green and lush were brown and dry around the whole county. Probably the whole state. Nonna took my glass and shooed me off to finish the weeding. I pulled my gloves back on and got back to it. The sun was unforgiving. It beat down on me in my t-shirt and jeans relentlessly. I hadn't seen a cloud in weeks. During the next hour, I made sure the unusually tiny sections of basil, oregano, fennel, chives, rosemary, thyme and sage were weeded and the wire fence to keep animals out was secure. Yes, we get all kinds of animals in New Jersey, deer, rabbits, squirrels, cats, crows, even the occasional black bear. I never understood those jokes about the New Jersey Turnpike. I mean, yes, there are seriously industrialized parts of the state, but it is also one of the country's leaders in many areas of farming. I lived in a suburb and only saw the turnpike when we went to the beach, which was maybe once a year. I ran my hand along the brittle leaves of a lemon verbena plant and walked to get the watering can. I used the last of the barrel of rainwater on the herbs, but it was nowhere near enough.

Scanning the sorry rows of tomatoes, peppers, zucchini and eggplant I shook my head. Usually, this garden was bursting with life. Bright colors and poignant fragrances. Not this year. Despite all the Novenas she prayed and the statues of St. Patrick and St. Fiacre that Uncle Vito added to the garden there had been no rain for weeks. It seemed as if there would be no end to this dry, hot summer. Nonna even had Fr. Verrell over twice to bless the statues and the garden itself. That night she was going over to our Church, the Church of the Sacred Heart, for a special Mass and as usual I would accompany her. In retrospect, I can say that Nonna seemed anxious. Tense even. Early that morning I had found her hanging several bundles of sage and fennel stalks in the kitchen on her drying rack before we left. Some bunches from our garden, but more she had bought. I should have guessed something was up then. Nonna never *bought* anything she could grow.

I always enjoyed going to Mass with Nonna. She kept a roll of cherry lifesavers in the huge black leather purse that she carried. After receiving Communion, she'd shove one of those sweet red candies at me. She whispered under her breath in a mixture of Latin, English and Italian. In her hands, she'd hold her ancient rope of rosary beads, made from black pearls worn smooth by years of prayer. When I was small she would let me hold them, and as I got older she showed me how to pray to the Virgin Mother. I was named after Mary, the Graziana part was a thank you to Mary that I was born happy and healthy. Nonna told me I should always be proud of my name. As long as I can remember, any time I even thought of Church I thought of cherry lifesavers and pearl rosary beads.

Some of the girls at school started wearing rosary beads as an accessory the first week of school. Sr. Diane put an end to that real fast. She held all of the female students after school in the library and had us research the origins of rosary beads and why they were not to be worn as decoration. Sacrilege if she ever saw it. Julianna was one of those girls, and she was not happy that her newest accessory was off limits. I happened to enjoy the research. I had never heard the story about a twelfth-century saint, Saint Dominic, who was given the first Rosary by an apparition of the Holy Virgin Mary. It was an amazing story. I have prayed the Rosary many times with my grandmother. Repeating the devotional prayers sometimes helped me to clear my mind. Whenever I thought of my parents and how much I missed them Nonna told me to pray. She believed praying would help me through my anger and my need for answers. I wasn't always so sure, but I tried.

After my weeding was finished, I headed inside for a shower. There wasn't much I could do to help the garden, but maybe a few prayers would help at Church. I was a little dubious, but I'd go. I mean praying was great, though my way was a little more unorthodox. It was like mental texting, but you know not to a friend from school or anything, to *God*. Or more often than not, to my parents, who according to Nonna, were angels in Heaven. You know, fighting the good fight against the devil and his minions. At the time, I had no idea that she actually meant that. When I prayed it usually went like this:

So yeah, it's me again. Idk if u have the time or anything, but if u could send a little rain this way to make Nonna happy I'd appreciate it. I miss u guys. Wish u were here, or I was there, but u know just for a visit. School is good. I got an A on my summer reading report. Btw I was looking at ur wedding photo today. I have it framed on my wall, it's so awesome. Mom u look like a movie star with all that make-up and sequins and lace and dad ur hair was soo long and blonde. I am still trying to figure out which one of you I look like. Nonna says I look like you mom. It's hard for me to see it tho. I wish you could answer me. I wish-, well anyway, I love you. Ttyl xoxo

It may sound lame, but I always felt like they could hear me. I crept upstairs trying to block out the yelling coming from my aunt and uncle's room. They had been fighting for months now. Aunt Theresa was always harping on him for one reason or another. Uncle Vito would rather be fiddling with his plants than trying to get into the Morris Garden Country Club which was just about all Aunt Theresa wanted out of life. It was a recurring fight. That and me of course. My mother was Uncle Vito's little sister, and he always had a smile and kind word for me. Aunt Theresa, on the other hand hated me. I never really understood why, but she pretty much ignored my existence. I wish her daughters would do the same. Rebecca was only ten and she was already a brat. Julianna hated me with a burning passion. Now I just tried to ignore them, but I didn't always feel that way. When they first moved in I was thrilled. I thought I would finally have a best friend, but Julianna despised me from the very second she laid her perfect blue eyes on me. I learned to hide that it hurt my feelings at a very early age.

That evening Nonna and I went to pray the Novena the Church was holding to end the drought. I love the smell of Church, incense and candles. The stained-glass windows gleamed after having been scrubbed, and I could smell the wood polish used on the curved, solid oak pews. The Church held a fundraiser a few years ago and had all of the pews reupholstered. Every August they were cleaned with a rug cleaner. I swear I could still smell the shampoo they used on the sturdy maroon fabric even though it had been cleaned weeks ago. I made sure the kneeler was down and Nonna and I knelt and got ready for the prayers to begin. I noticed Fr. Verrell had a new priest on the altar with him. He was young*ish* for a priest, in his late thirties maybe. He was blonde haired and blue eyed. He didn't speak during services, but his gaze never seemed to leave us. I thought it must be because I was the only person there under sixty. Nonna had gone rigid at the sight of him.

"Maria, pass me the prayer book," I did as she asked, but wondered why she needed one. Nonna knew the Rosary by heart. She never missed a Mass or prayer service. I watched her as she refused to make eye contact with the altar. I had never seen her like this. She spent the rest of Mass purposely ignoring the new priest. Now, normally she'd seek out new members of the clergy and introduce herself and invite them over for a Sunday dinner, but not this time. After Mass ended she grabbed my hand and pulled me outside to wait for Uncle Vito. We didn't even wait in line to speak to Fr. Verrell. I shrugged, she must be really worried about the damage the drought was doing to the garden. I didn't know any better yet.

2

The next Monday started like any other Monday except it was hot. *Super hot*. Sweat was trickling down my back between my white cotton sports bra and the hideous synthetic uniform we all wore to school. The boys got to wear khaki pants and white or yellow golf shirts. Not too bad, right? The girls had to wear stiff white Oxford blouses tucked into a brown and yellow plaid skirt and a brown snap tie. Knee high brown socks and penny loafers completed this fashion disaster. Sr. Diane actually took a ruler out some days to check the hemline of our skirts. No more than one inch above the knee was tolerated. For many girls that meant a trip to the ladies' room to unroll their skirts, and for the rest, they had to tear out their too short hemlines and spend the morning in home economics to re-sew them. I never had this problem of course. My hemline came just past my knees, and I could care less. No one here noticed me anyway. Except for Julianna, and believe me, I could do without the notice.

Fourth period that day was Phys. Ed. *Oh joy, oh rapture.* Because they shifted my classes around so I could take English and Math with the juniors that meant I also had Phys. Ed. with them. I freely admit a complete lack of coordination and a general unease at the thought of all things sports-like. Let's just say that when it came to our high school physical education class, I was in my least comfort zone. The locker room was the worst. Especially when Julianna and the cheering squad came in. When they got changed, they weren't like the rest of us hurrying into our even more hideous gym uniforms. Ill-fitting brown shorts that again came to our knees and white t-shirts that were so cheap they were see through. The school logo was printed in brown across our chests. The logo was supposed to be a Zephyr, you know like a whirlwind, but it just looked like a splatter of mud.

So, there I was about to change into my mud shirt and shorts, possibly the most unbecoming outfit of all time, when I looked up to see the cheerleaders. Julianna was cheer captain. Quite an achievement for a junior, usually the position was reserved for a senior. The whole team was converged on the other side of the row of faded pink lockers. They wore matching hot pink and green leopard printed bras and practically nonexistent underwear. A bunch of them were pointing and laughing at the girl next to me.

Angela Tanner. She was a junior like them, but *not* like them. That was the point. Unlike her perfectly highlighted, tanned and size zero classmates, Angela's skin was so pale you could see her blue veins running through her arms and legs, except for the spots covered by orange freckles. They matched the short spiral curls that shot up all over her head. She was also a girl who appreciated food. Now when it came to eating I was not a slacker, I just never seemed to gain a pound. Angela would have been a total bombshell in the fifties, like a Betty Grable or Virginia Mayo, but nowadays starvation seemed to be all the rage. To Julianna and her cronies being anything over a hundred and fifteen pounds was the equivalent of being a leper. I had only spoken to Angela a few times, but she was a nice girl. She wrote for the school e-newspaper and took photos for the yearbook. Her dad was super rich, but she was down to earth. Sometimes we rode the bus together.

"Hey Angela, where do you get like panties that big? You shop at that fatty store, don't you? You know the one, Julianna, the old lady one that like my granny shops at?!" Jennifer, a petite blonde clone of my cousin's, high-fived another girl and laughed as Angela struggled to get her shorts and shirt on before turning her back to grab her sneakers. Her face was bright pink with humiliation.

"Hey, Angela *need-to-get* Tanner! We're talking to you!" Julianna laughed again and continued getting dressed. Angela kept her head down and ignored the bitchy comments the cheerleaders made. I tried not to notice as a tear rolled down her cheek. It made my stomach turn. I shot my cousin a dirty look which only caused her to focus on me. Normally, I wouldn't have drawn attention to myself. But I was not feeling great that day. It was just so hot, and I must have been getting ready for *that time.* Seeing them pick on Angela just rubbed me the wrong way.

"Knock it off, Julianna." I looked over while still in my sports bra and a pair of plain white boy-shorts.

"OMG ladies, do you see this? Hey freak, where did you get the boy's underwear? From a real boy? I didn't know you, like, knew any." More pointing and laughing. This time at me, as they donned their shorts and shirts they rolled them up and tucked them in until they actually looked good. *Damn it.*

"Leave me alone, clones," I said and turned to quickly get into my shorts and shirt. I tied my ancient Nikes and ignored them as, long limbed and golden tanned, the cheerleaders swept past me in a cloud of cotton candy perfume and makeup.

"Yeah right! Next time keep out of our business. Oops!" Julianna walked past and knocked my bottled water under a locker. More snickering followed my cousin's latest display of teen bullying. *Bravo to you Jules, you really take the cake.*

"I have an extra," Angela held a bottle of spring water out to me though she couldn't quite meet my eyes.

"Thanks, and uh, I'm sorry about my cousin. You know what they say, you can't pick family."

"True." She shrugged her shoulders and pulled her wayward curls back in a glittery yellow headband.

"Anyway, she's just a little bit full of herself."

"Yeah, we'll if I looked like her I'd be full of myself too. You know where my mom sent me this summer? To fat camp! That's right, six weeks of dieting and exercising and, know what? I lost *three* pounds. Yup, that's right, three whole pounds. Mom was devastated of course, but it's not my fault. I have a hormonal imbalance, and it is really hard for me to lose the weight. They told me not to eat carbs! *Don't eat carbs?* I'm sixteen, of course, I want to eat freaking carbs!" Angela sighed and attempted to tuck her cell phone into her pocket, but it was a hopeless endeavor. She threw it in her locker and slammed the door.

"She's not perfect, you know. That's the benefit of being related to her. I know stuff. You know she'd kill me if I told anyone this but when she was in seventh grade, she was a hundred and sixty pounds and had acne. Like bad acne." I held up my hands to show the monster sized pimples Julianna had had all over her face and back.

"I'd love to get my hands on any pictures you have! For the yearbook! LOL" We both laughed. I guess having a common enemy does make friends out of strangers.

Because the weather was good albeit hot, we were going outside for class. We started running laps around the track that circled the new turf soccer field. Coach Vinnie timed us on his old digital stopwatch. He wore his usual royal blue matching running suit sans jacket and white golf shirt. Huge rings of sweat circled his armpits and chest. He kept chugging from an orange Gatorade bottle. I couldn't blame him, it was hot.

Angela and I stayed to the back of the group, away from the star athletes and cheerleaders. My eyes kept flashing ahead though. To *him*. Sebastian De La Cruz, starting forward of the SHPS Zephyrs Soccer Team, state champs three years running, was leading the pack. Julianna was running close behind him. She was doing it mostly to get a look at his butt. She'd been hinting all summer that this year he'd be taking her to prom. In her world, the star cheerleader belonged with the star athlete. At our school that meant Sebastian or Sebby, as he was commonly known, and Julianna.

Sebastian was just about the most perfect boy I had ever seen. He was pretty tall, about five-foot eleven, which was even tall for me and I'm five-foot nine. Lean and muscular, a true soccer player's build. He must have been outdoors a lot during the summer because his clear skin was a gorgeous golden tan. His black hair was cut short and he ran with effortless grace. He was beautiful to watch. I had to agree with Julianna there. But he was far out of my league. I knew I'd never win a beauty contest and I was more likely to read a book than put on make-up and style my hair. I couldn't help it, nothing I did would change how I looked anyway. I was almost sixteen, but I looked about three years younger. My dark brown hair hung down my back in a single braid and my eyes were a boring brown. I was too tall to be cute and too bony to be really attractive, so I didn't try.

Sebastian held the lead with a few of his soccer buddies. Mike was shorter and stockier than Sebby. He had wavy blonde hair and freckles. He was a tough player. He held all sorts of goalie records in the state. Tyler was tall, dark haired and not very cute. He had a big nose and an acne problem, but girls still drooled over him. Probably because he hung around with Sebby. Julianna, Lizette, Jennifer and a couple of other cheerleaders would intermittently jog up to them then they would stop to stretch. Although who really needed to stretch every fifteen minutes while jogging laps? It was really just an excuse to stick out their chests in their push up bras and bend over to show off their legs and such. *Whatever. Way to be subtle, ladies.*

In the middle of my third lap, my head started pounding. The trees around the new turf field started blending into one another. The sun was so bright I couldn't look at the sky. I blinked several times, trying to clear my line of vision, but it was as if I could only focus on the most minuscule thing. Like the tiny pieces of rubber turf dotting the track or the piece of blue lint sticking to my shoelace. I blinked again and shook my head a little. The temperature was rising. I could feel my uniform clinging to me and my throat closing in. I tried to suck in more of the dry air, but it was as if the heat was pressing in on me. I slowed down and doubled over, struck by a cramp. My stomach was turning in on itself. I felt my heart pounding away inside of me. *Thump, thump, thump.* I had never felt such intense pain. As if my insides were trying to claw their way out.

"Ms. Kelly? Come on, on your feet, kiddo. Kelly? Hey!" Coach Vinnie yelled, but I couldn't move. He blew his whistle, and I could feel everyone look at me. I could hear their whispers, but I couldn't make a sound. Like I was trapped in my own personal bubble of heat and pain.

"Omg what a freak!"

"Hey girl, that's your cousin, right?"

"So, what, it's not like we're like friends or anything." I could hear Julianna's stiff reply.

"Don't you, like have to live with her? It's so good of your mom and dad to let her live with you!"

"Yeah well, uh, my dad's a bleeding heart. Not my choice, believe me." I knew how being related to me wasn't something she openly shared. Must have ticked her off that someone put it all together. Right then I didn't really care, my stomach was in a vice grip.

"What's the matter with her? You know, besides the obvious."

"Little Orphan Annie, is trying to get sympathy points I guess, jeez Jules. She is such a loser."

"Yeah, you're so right, Jen! She is so jealous of you, Jules, look at her trying to get pity points or whatever."

"Ugh. Whatever." Julianna said through clenched teeth, I could feel her eyeing me with disgust.

"Ms. Kelly, you okay," Coach Vinnie was next to me trying to get me up. I couldn't move, I was in the grips of a pain I had never felt. "You're burning up. She's burning up gang, back up a few steps, please. Move it! Julianna, come here, this is your cousin, right?" He didn't wait for a reply which was a good thing, she might have denied it. "Listen up, I want you to go get the nurse. Tell her to come here right away and you might want to call home."

"Um, yeah I would, but-"

"I'll go," I think it was Tyler and he ran inside to alert Nurse Carol.

Their voices sounded foggy and unclear, as if I were underwater. I vaguely recall the nurse coming and taking my temperature. Someone poured water into my mouth. It was cold, it felt wonderful going down my burning throat. Strong, gentle hands helped me to my feet. My legs shook beneath me. Someone prompted me to walk. I recognized Angela on one side of me. She held my arm and looked worried. I stumbled as another cramp hit me. Someone else slid an arm around me. I inhaled. It was pleasant. *Sebastian.* His strong arm held me upright. The two of them walked me to the nurse's office. They helped me lay down on the tan pleather chaise. Sebastian waited while Angela fetched a cool washcloth for my head. I could smell the fresh laundry scent of him even as I clutched my stomach. I knew I would be mortified the next time I saw him, but right then I didn't care. It was all I could do not to be sick all over the floor in front of him.

"Hey, you're gonna be ok," he said with a quiet strength that comforted me. Angela returned and placed the washcloth on my forehead. It felt wonderful. Nurse Carol, a short, stocky woman in her mid-fifties with gray streaked blonde hair and a no-nonsense attitude, soon shooed them off to class.

"Ms. Kelly, I've called your house and your grandmother said your uncle is on his way, okay? Just hang in there, honey." Her voice was calm, but I could tell by the sound of her voice she was worried. Clearly, she had no idea what was wrong with me. I heard her whispering into the phone from the hallway. "Well, yes, she is burning up, but she also appears to have pain in her abdomen. No, not appendicitis. It's more centered. Yes, ok. No, her parents are deceased, no I'll tell her grandmother, ok. Thank you." By the time my uncle came to get me the pain in my stomach had started to fade. I still felt feverish and I could hardly move. I felt so tired. Used up. Like I had run thirty miles instead of three little laps.

"Hey kiddo, you okay?" Uncle Vito asked as we drove home in his pick-up truck. I nodded and laid back, eyes closed. When they were open it was like I could see every microscopic detail in front of me. A bead of sweat on my uncle's brow, a speck of dirt on the car mat that was actually a dead bug, a piece of a fry he must have eaten for lunch stuck between his teeth. It was all too much. I closed my eyes to get away from it, but the noise. *Ouch.* Uncle Vito had loads of gardening tools in the back, they clanged around as he drove. I tried to keep my breaths shallow, but the noise was intense. I could *smell* everything also. Soil, grass, fertilizer, coffee, hand sanitizer, my uncle's aftershave. Not bad smells. Familiar and even pleasant somehow. But they were *strong.*

Uncle Vito was a big guy, tall and good looking. His dark hair was streaked with some gray and his brown eyes always twinkled with mischief. He was forever pulling gags like tugging Nonna's apron strings open while she cooked dinner or hiding behind the door to scare Rebecca when she came down the stairs. Stuff like that. Stuff that Julianna and Aunt Theresa no longer seemed to appreciate. His landscaping business was taking some hard hits with this drought, and I felt bad for him. I was determined not to be a burden. I could already feel the guilt Aunt Theresa would heap on me for making my uncle miss a job to come and get me. Not that she could miss her weekly hair appointment to get me herself. Before we pulled into the driveway I could see Nonna. She waited for me with a glass in her hand. Her medicinal tea, already iced and in my favorite tall blue glass. Her special blend of tea and herbs to make me feel better no matter what ailed me. I knew it would be sweet with honey and a little lemon. To brighten it, she always said. I asked her how to make it every once in a while, but she always waved me away. One day she would leave me all her recipes, she promised.

"*Cara Mia*, how are you feeling? Okay now?" The anxiety on her face a stark contrast with her usual quiet reassurance.

"I'm fine Nonna, I just have some cramps, and I think maybe a little fever." I took a sip of the iced tea and walked inside. I knew she would make me finish it all before I could go to my room so I sat down at the kitchen table and forced myself to drink it. The sweet familiar taste I expected was bitter and hard to swallow. I gagged a little only to be met with a cross stare from

Nonna. She pointed at the cup, an indication for me to drink and continued talking to Uncle Vito in quick southern Italian dialect. I knew he was anxious to leave. Aunt Theresa would be back soon and he'd rather be gone. I didn't blame him.

"Thanks, Uncle Vito," He rubbed my head and said goodbye. He wasn't very demonstrative in his affections. A good pat on the head was like a declaration of love from him. I smiled.

"No problem, kiddo, just feel better," he smiled back at me and turned to put his worn-out Yankees cap on his head. He kissed his mother on the cheek and hurried out the door.

"Okay now, you finish your tea? Maria, drink it all. No wasting time. Please, *cara*."

It was the please that did it. Nonna rarely used that word. She didn't have to. She was the best cook in the whole state. There wasn't a drink or dish anyone wouldn't gladly finish and ask for more. Maybe it was the fever, but for the first time I couldn't swallow another drop.

"Sure, I'm going to finish it." Another white lie for me to confess to Fr. Verrell next week.

"Good girl."

I watched as she walked to the stove stirring the big pot of what smelled like her famous chicken soup. She used fresh organic chicken breast, sweet onions, celery and fresh plump carrots. I could smell dill and parsley and the familiar olive oil she used in everything. It gave it flavor, she always said. I waited for her to start singing. Frank Sinatra this time, he was one of her favorites. *Fly me to the moon.*

It's not often I disobey Nonna, but I couldn't force another swallow of that tea down. I poured it in the small potted house plant that sat in its customary spot in the center of the scarred oak table. That table had been in my Nonna's kitchen since she moved here in the 1970s with my grandfather. He passed away years ago, I knew he built this table and she loved it.

"I'm gonna go upstairs and lay down. Thanks, Nonna," I said and hurried out of the room after placing my cup in the sink. I was a terrible liar. I knew she would sniff it out of me in a second if she asked me if I finished my tea again.

My head started to pound as I took the stairs slowly up to my room. My room used to be the attic and I had the whole floor to myself. Uncle Vito put in a large bay window and window seat overlooking the backyard. It helped me not to feel cramped. I had adequate space even though the ceiling sloped on one side. I was able to fit a small futon that served as a couch and bed for a guest and a full-sized bed for myself. Uncle Vito and I painted the walls a pale buttercup yellow and the ceiling was white. The colors helped make the room look bigger. Julianna and Rebecca shared a room and I was sincerely grateful for my own space. I had my own bathroom, complete with a full-size tub, rubber duck printed shower curtain and rug. I liked rubber ducks.

I have a collection of rubber ducks on an old wooden shelf in the corner of my room. My mom started it for me when I was a baby. I have football ducks, rock star ducks, ducks painted like dragons and fairies. Even the quilt on my bed had rubber ducks all over it. I didn't remember much about my parents, but I kept every duck they ever gave me. A small pink one was my favorite. My mom got it for me the day she found out she was going to have a little girl. Since then it's been a little tradition in the family. Every Christmas I get a duck in my stocking, every Easter one in my basket and last year for my birthday Nonna made me a cake in the shape of a giant rubber duck. Yellow buttercream and all. But that day my little ducks gave me no comfort.

I went straight to the air conditioner the minute I closed my door. It was on full blast, but I couldn't feel it at all. I peeled off my sweaty gym clothes and worked the shower till I stood under a sharp spray of cold water. Some minutes later, I'm not sure how many, I got out of the shower and put on my cotton bathrobe. I didn't even run a brush through my hair, I had no energy. *Zero. Zip.* I collapsed on my bed without turning the covers down or changing into pajamas.

That night as I slept I had the dream again. My mother was still fuzzy. I couldn't make out her face or her body. Only her hair when it tickled my cheek and her scent was clear to me. I wanted to reach up and hold her, but my arms were too heavy. I couldn't move them no matter how hard I tried. I started to call out, but it was as if my voice wouldn't work. My mind screamed for her to stay, to help me, but I couldn't make a sound. The next morning, I woke up to her shouting the same phrase at me over and over, "Run Maria, run! Run!" I felt completely unrefreshed and unsettled when I stumbled into my bathroom. On top of that, I was late. I looked at my haggard reflection and quickly washed my face and brushed my teeth. *What the heck? How did I get leaves in my hair?* I looked around and saw the window was open, no wonder it was so hot. I shut the window and hastily dressed. I could still make the school bus, but I had to skip breakfast which stunk because I was starving.

"Late today aren't you," Aunt Theresa said as she looked me up and down. My uniform shirt was wrinkled and untucked, and my socks were slouched around my ankles. I knew Julianna would be crisp and perfect, but what can I say. We had serious differences about what was important in life.

"You really don't care what people think of this family do you, Maria Graziana? Your poor uncle being dragged off of work to get you and you can't even brush your hair. I doubt you were even sick. You're never sick. Not even when we all had the flu last year. Just grasping for attention! You are spoiled rotten." My aunt's eyes raked over me, and I cringed. I knew how she saw me and she wasn't wrong. I haven't been sick since I was a little girl and I never tried hard with my appearance. What for? One look at my cousin as she appeared in the doorway and I knew it would never make a difference anyway. Julianna's hair was done in an intricate waterfall braid with perfect wisps framing her peaches and cream complexion. Her baby doll blue eyes were outlined with brown eyeliner and mascara and her pouty mouth glossed over in the faintest of pinks. Minimal makeup was allowed at our school, though some girls did go overboard. Not Julianna. She had personal appearance down to an art. *Kudos to you, cuz.*

My own hair was in a low ponytail and hung down my back since I didn't have time to do anything more than brush it. As for my complexion, it was clear and tanned from my time in the garden and maybe a little oily since I couldn't seem to stop sweating. No make-up though. Not now and probably not ever since I had no idea how to apply it. Julianna's hair was about a dozen different colors from brown to pale blonde. She had it highlighted every eight weeks. It was quite pretty. Even her little sister Rebecca was beginning to show what a beauty she would be. Big blue eyes like her sister and curly light brown hair. Of course, my hair was a dull dark brown, and wavy which meant it never curled or straightened completely. It was also too long. When I let it loose, it fell past my waist. Nonna wasn't one of those older women into getting her hair done every week. In fact, she hardly noticed her hair and got it cut at the same barber who cut my grandfather's hair once a month. When I was little I would wait to be asked to join my cousins and aunt on one of their salon trips, but I never was. It hurt me then.

Nowadays Aunt Theresa told me I should cut my hair almost constantly. Maybe that's why I refused to. I didn't have the time or the inclination that morning to care about the vast difference in beauty between my cousin and me. We had a test in Lit and I was sure I wouldn't do well since I slept all the previous day and didn't even start my homework. *Crap.* I hated that. Hated being unprepared.

"Good morning Aunt Theresa," was all I had said before Nonna walked in.

"Maria, you don't go to school today, you were sick yesterday, remember?" Her housedress was streaked with dirt where she rubbed her fingers after picking something from the garden. She held purple flowers with dark green leaves and a piece of root in her hands. I didn't recognize any of it. Weird, considering I had worked the garden since I could hold a trowel.

"I have to, Nonna, I have a test today," I kissed her cheek and headed out the door. Julianna was there already and promptly ignored me as we took seats on opposite sides of the bus. I found Angela on the bus and sat down next to her. I opened my school bag to take a sip from my water bottle only to find Nonna had replaced my usual iced water with that weird tea from yesterday. I choked down the gulp I took and quickly closed the cap. I'd throw it out at school.

"Hey girl, so, how are you? I was worried after you keeled over like that in gym yesterday." Angela moved her backpack off the seat next to her and I slumped into the chair. Today she had a big purple headband holding her bright orange curls at bay. It was cute in a fairy-punk sort of way.

"Yeah, that was weird. I don't know, I like slept for ten hours, but I'm fine now." I shrugged.

"Really? Wow! When I'm sick, it takes me days to recover!" I listened to Angela go on about her latest bout with seasonal allergies and tried to ignore the giggling coming from Julianna and her friends.

"Hey Maria," said Lizette, a short dark-haired version of my cousin, complete with waterfall braid and perfectly applied make-up. "You should like buy some Midol for those super cramps of yours. That is if you're old enough to get your period. You do know what that is, sweetie, don't you?"

"Sure, she gets her period, just started last week in fact."

"Well, maybe she forgot how to be a girl under those guy clothes she wears," more laughter.

"Hey Grazi, where do you get your underwear? My little brother wants to know!"

I wanted to disappear. My cousin was such a jerk. Julianna knew that I had only gotten my period the previous summer. Three years after she had hers. Apparently, she thought it was cool to blab about it to her clones. My head started pounding, and I closed my eyes. I could hear my heartbeat, perspiration was beading on my forehead. I took a tissue out of my backpack and wiped it quickly. Trying to ignore the sounds behind me. Angela gave me a sympathetic smile but ducked her head and pretended to read something on her cellphone before anyone could see her. I couldn't blame her. She was being harassed enough on her own. The cheerleading squad was the Sacred Heart Preparatory School's own personal torture squad. Their job was to flaunt themselves and their physical perfection in front of us lesser mortals, to berate, humiliate, and embarrass us. So basically, they were designed to just make us all sick. Julianna discussing my personal life shouldn't have surprised me, but still it hurt.

I was sensitive about my lack of development. Even Rebecca, who was barely eleven, was starting to wear training bras. Nonna took me to the pediatrician after my fourteenth birthday came and went and still no period. He said I was fine. A picture of health. In fact, he attributed my late menstruation to the fact that unlike most children I was raised on a mostly organic diet since birth. Especially meats and dairy. He said that the hormones in regular products caused the early onset of menstruation and physical development in most young girls these days and that I was not abnormal at all. My mom always bought organic and after I had moved in with Nonna, she did too.

Aunt Theresa liked to cook her own food and she

didn't believe in it. She thought Nonna was just spoiling me. After I turned fifteen my menstrual cycle started and, seriously, a year has passed and I still don't see what the rush is. I could have gone a few more years without it. I mean who the heck wants to start their cycle anyway? I understand it is necessary for the propagation of the species, but it is uncomfortable if not downright painful. *Cramps, bloating, mood swings, ugh.* Having your period sucks. I can only imagine what childbirth will be like if this is the precursor to it. Nonna said that was why we're the stronger sex because if men had to do it they simply wouldn't.

"Jeez," Angela said and peeked over at my cousin, "How can you stand living with her?"

"No choice."

"Yeah well, at least she'll be gone in two years, right? College."

"Yeah, college." Not very likely. Julianna had other aspirations. She was determined to be the next Teen Idol. Rumor had it the show was headed to New Jersey for auditions in a few years. Her big chance. *Go, Julianna! Seriously, go.*

As soon as I got through homeroom, I headed for the cafeteria. My stomach was rumbling loudly and I was more than a little embarrassed. Especially after the whole period thing on the bus. I got on the small line and chose a bowl of oatmeal, an organic banana, and because I hadn't had any dinner the night before I swiped a side of Cherry Blossom Farms organic turkey bacon too. I felt better after the bacon and managed to get through the rest of my day.

3

The week went by quickly after that. I didn't do as bad as I thought on my Lit test. In fact, I aced it. I have a knack for essay questions. Even if I don't really know the answer, I have a way of writing that my teachers seem to like. I just tell them what I do know and they go for it. Mrs. Theodore is harder than most to get over on, but she couldn't find error with my work. I was really relieved. I needed to keep my grades up to get into a good college and earn a scholarship. It was important to me, the idea that I would go to a good school, *one that was far away*, get a degree, a good job and live a happy and productive life.

By Friday morning the heat had become just about unbearable. I spent hours after school the day before weeding our garden and trying to give what little water we were allowed to the herbs and plants that were most likely to benefit from it. I felt guilty for the long shower I had when I was feeling ill the other day. After dinner that night I stacked lawn and leaf bags full of dry brittle debris from the yard onto the curb for pick up. It was becoming clearer that the entire tri-state area was suffering from this drought.

The state government was trying to get approved to airlift water from neighboring states to the more important fields of corn and grain that were as of now burning in the brutal sun day after day with no relief in sight. In our hometown, local carwashes were forced to close and people were tense as supermarket prices continued to rise on veggies and fruits. As usual half of the air conditioning at school wasn't working and they gave us a "dress down" day. That usually meant jeans and t-shirts, but for Julianna and the cheering clones it meant summer dresses with crisscross backs and little button up short sleeve cardigans since spaghetti straps were off limits. And of course, the hairstyle of the day was a fishtail braid turned up into a clip with clever little wisps around the face. My hair was in a messy bun on top of my head and I had on my usual Levi's and a t-shirt that said "Go Green" with a picture of Yoda on the back.

I walked into the school library and expected to see Sister Marcia. She was about ninety years old, a sister of Charity, and the school librarian. Instead of the familiar white and gray habited nun sitting in her old leather chair with her traditional steaming mug of tea, a slight blonde woman in a beige tank dress was in her place. She was almost painfully thin with large gray eyes and a small unsmiling mouth. She was unpacking a box of books.

"Um, hi," The woman gasped and dropped the box cutter she was using.

"Ooh, you scared me," She looked at me and smiled, a small frightened looking smile and I felt bad immediately. She was so small she looked as if she'd fall over if I even breathed on her.

"Oh, I'm sorry. I'm Grazi Kelly, I usually help Sr. Marcia with the library books during this period."

"Oh yes, she left me a note about you. Maria Graziana, right? Well um, hello, I'm Ms. Vorax. I'm filling in this marking period for Sr. Marcia. She's having hip replacement surgery. It's so nice to meet you, I understand you are earning your service points for Confirmation by helping out in here, is that right?" I shook the small, fragile hand. I didn't mean to stare, but I couldn't help it. I felt like I recognized her.

"Yeah, I mean I'd help anyway, but we are required

to perform twenty-five community service hours in order to meet our requirement to make Confirmation in the spring. Oh, I have a sheet here you are supposed to sign for me whenever I come in." I handed her the sheet. She nodded and took out a pen. She wrote her name in careful and precise letters. She reminded me of when my cousin, Rebecca, first learned how to write in script. As if she just learned too, silly of me I guess.

"I'm sorry, but you look familiar, did you sub here before?"

"Um no, no I haven't." Her hands shook as she reached for the box cutter again. Then it hit me. The big eyes, the nervous expression, I knew where I had seen her. Her face was plastered on the news the second half of the summer! She was the sole survivor of a horrible camping disaster that happened over the summer.

Two hikers got lost on the Kittatinny Range, a pretty popular Appalachian trail that crosses the Delaware River. They were missing for over ten days during one of the summer's heat waves. Temperatures were over 100 degrees for days. People speculated the pair got lost in one of the bogs or fell off a steep, rocky pitch somewhere. It was later reported their camp was attacked by some kind of black or brown bear. Ms. Vorax survived, but her companion was apparently killed and eaten by the animal in a gruesome attack.

I didn't know what to do, or what to say so I just put down my school bag and started helping her go through the box. We worked quietly for a few minutes then students started coming in. Ms.Vorax kept her head down and when a freshman boy came in with a question, she was forced to face the students.

"Hi, Can you help me with this? I'm supposed to get information on the Revolutionary War that comes from an actual book?" John Kercheck, the freshman, looked at the teacher, then he started waving his hand around like a complete idiot. "Oooh, Ooh, I know you! Wow! Yeah, you're that lady! The survivor from the Sunfish Pond bear attack!" Ms. Vorax stopped and looked down panic quickly spreading over her. I couldn't believe his complete lack of manners and disregard for her feelings.

"Hey John, you want that section right there. Non-fiction, history, it's separated by country then by year. Thanks." I pushed him along and stood guard over the new librarian. Most students had their own laptops, so they didn't need much help. But for the ones that *did*, I fielded questions and helped the new freshman learn how to use the library system and the one computer we had in the corner.

"I'm sorry you had to be put through that. You probably don't like to talk about it." I didn't look directly at her as I spoke, sometimes it's just easier to say things that way.

"Oh my goodness, I have got to get it together. Thank you so much, Maria. I just wasn't expecting- I mean you're right I don't. I don't mean to be rude, but I lost one of my best friends. It was horrible losing her like that, you can't imagine. The violence, the blood, I'm sorry, Maria, I can't talk about it."

"No, it's okay. I mean, I understand. Please call me, Grazi." The tears in her eyes made me ashamed of that dopey freshman. I couldn't imagine having such a terrible experience and I was almost glad I had no close friends to lose. Almost. I turned my head to give her a minute to pull herself together. She used a tissue to blot under her large gray eyes and pasted a bright smile on her face. It was fake, but I wasn't going to call her on it. She'd been through enough. The reporters harassed her through her rescue and recovery in the hospital, I figured she earned her privacy.

"Okay Grazi, why don't you start shelving these books? I already entered them in the library database, and I will finish opening these boxes, okay?"

"Sure." I smiled at her and headed toward the stack of new books. We worked in companionable silence for the next forty minutes. I was more interested in the selection I was shelving than in talking anyway. Several books on the history of the Catholic Church, patron saints and where they lived, religion and war, a history of popes. One book grabbed my interest. It wasn't new like the others. It was big, leather bound, its pages edged in gold. I glanced at the title, <u>Mysticism, Legends, and Folk Tales: A History</u>. No author listed. I was sure Sr. Marcia would have never let that book through the door much less put it on a shelf. I was super curious.

"No, no, not that one. That's personal research, um, for my thesis," Ms. Vorax moved with more speed and strength than I would have given her slight frame credit for. She took the heavy book from my hands. It disappeared under the desk. I'll admit I didn't think about it again. I took it as she said, it was for her own research project, not school property, and therefore, not my business. Besides, I felt bad that the horror story that happened to her over the summer had been thrown up in her face on her very first day at work. I felt embarrassed and a little protective. In any case, I just wanted to finish shelving the books in silence.

I never had to worry about tripping over my tongue with Sr. Marcia. It was kind of exhausting doing so now. *I should probably send her a get-well card.* I distracted myself with thoughts of my old librarian. I missed her off-key humming. She would constantly hum Church hymns while we worked. It left little room for chit chat. Sometimes she would ask after my grandmother and family and sometimes she brought up things my mother did when she attended this very same school. But that was as far as it went with Sr. Marcia.

I missed her today and realized I appreciated the boundaries the older nun had set up between herself and the students. I looked over at the tiny and fragile Ms. Vorax and wondered how soon before the rest of the school found out who she was. As it turned out not very long at all. Everyone was talking about our temporary librarian and the hiking trip that ended in the gruesome death of her best friend, Estella Ramirez. By last period I had heard it so many times I thought I would scream. It was terrible and tragic, and it was real. It wasn't some B horror flick! I wished they could just leave it alone and respect Ms. Vorax's privacy.

"I heard they only found pieces of that other hiker."

"Yeah, like a Nike and some chewed on rib bones."

"They never found the bear either."

"I heard she spent the rest of the summer in a nut house."

More snickering and rude comments were made as I walked to the bus stop. Three o'clock. You could tell the time by how many girls were sprinting down the hallway and outside, sweaters off showing tanned shoulders and cleavage. Some took off their flirty dresses and revealed skimpy bikini tops and cutoffs. The boys followed after them of course. Like puppies, helpless to resist what they saw as a treat. They all laughed and talked about the pool party at Lizette's house after school. Not surprisingly, I was *not* invited.

The bus was late which made not being invited to the pool party even more humiliating. I was probably one of ten people not going. I turned and noticed that new priest, Fr. Gallagher. He was standing outside of the school in a white-collared black short sleeve shirt, the summer uniform for priests. His arms were crossed as he looked around campus. I supposed he was making sure everyone was behaving accordingly. His gaze found mine, and he nodded. I turned around and kept walking. He was a little too intense for me.

I spent that weekend helping Nonna, attending Mass, and doing homework. Sleep was hard to come by in the unbearable heat so I spent the hours reading and listening to music. I had an old tape of my mom's that I found in the attic closet when I was twelve. It was a mixed tape and I had since downloaded most of the songs onto my iPod. My mom loved a lot of different types of music. She had everything from dance, to hip hop, early rap, old rock and roll, and alternative. My favorites were the eighties punk bands, like The Ramones. I felt closer to her when I listened to the music she did at my age. I googled the lyrics and had them committed to memory. Maybe I thought knowing her favorite music would help me be closer to her. I don't know. It made me feel better and that was worth it I guess.

By Monday morning news of our school librarian was dying down. I headed over to return some books and say hi to Ms. Vorax. I stopped in the doorway. The cheerleaders and some members of the football team were standing there chatting and gathering some tools and things.

"Here, let's hang this arrowhead vine from my daddy's greenhouse over your desk Ms. Vorax." I guess Julianna was showing extra school spirit by sprucing up the library. But a plant from her "daddy's greenhouse" when she never even bothered to go to Uncle Vito's office never mind the small greenhouse where he grew specialized plants, flowers and shrubs. Maybe she was going to run for student council or something. Anyways, I looked around and was shocked at what the addition of a few hanging plants and framed museum posters could do. Sure, I helped organize and stack books but I never would have thought of this. Watching Julianna give Ms. Vorax a fake little hug and air kiss was about as much as I could take. *What a phony!* I mean, considering my cousin had never, to my knowledge, entered the school library before. I turned around and walked out unnoticed.

The temperature was in the nineties and the student body was vocal about their discomfort. The amount of groaning during class had increased by at least twenty percent.

"Heads up!" Several illegal water balloons were thrown during lunch period. Of course, I got hit right in the head and had to spend my entire history class with Mr. Gundy taking frequent glances at me. Not that I could blame him, my hair and uniform were soaking wet. I was grateful I had on a tank top underneath my blouse or it would have been completely transparent.

I had Phys. Ed. last period and was changing as quickly as possible before Julianna, and her clones came into the locker room. Angela was already changed and took a seat next to me while I tied my sneakers.

"Grazi, have you heard about that old guy?"

"Hmm? What old guy?"

"That 7-11 guy, from Old Broadway Road? He's been missing for days! They found him last night behind the dumpster in the back of the 7-11 parking lot!"

"Oh no! What happened to him?"

"Daddy gets his newspaper there in the mornings before driving to his office, you know, in Manhattan. Anyway, he called me from his cell and said there were like ten cop cars and they were picking him up in little *baggies*! He knows I'd be interested for *NewsFlash*. You know I'm junior editor this year, right? Anyway, I'm gonna do a small write up in, like a memorial/crime piece." *NewsFlash* is the official Sacred Heart Prep e-news site. Students wrote articles, posted photographs and videos of current events around the school, church, and surrounding neighborhoods. Since Catholic schools tended to be small we had a lot of kids come in from other suburbs and towns. I noticed Angela had a faraway look on her face. No doubt she was writing the piece in her head already.

I couldn't believe what had happened. That was the 7-11 where Nonna and I stopped for lottery tickets and cherry slurpees all the time. I *knew* that old man. Nonna used to tell me how he moved here with his family from India twenty years ago for a better life. She said it was amazing and I should be proud that I lived in a country where people would leave everything they had ever known just to have a chance to live here. I never thought of it till now. I remember he used to give me candy when I was younger, small butterscotches wrapped in gold foil. I used to think they were treasure. I didn't even know his name. Angela was still talking, and since I wanted to know more, I figured I should pay attention.

"Yeah, my Dad was so bummed. Now, they're going to be closed for like ever and he'll have to drive all the way to the Quick Check for his paper. It's like an extra seven minutes in the car. I mean I know it's horrible and all. Oh no, Grazi, you must think I'm such a jerk! Really, I mean I am sorry and all..."

I clenched my jaw. Angela was saying something else to me, but I couldn't hear her. I made a gesture not to worry and we stood up and walked out of the locker room. Sweat trickled down my spine. The sun blazed above us, there wasn't a cloud in sight. I remembered to apply sunblock earlier that morning I just hoped I hadn't sweated it all off already. The class was congregated by the Coach, and I could hear him going through the roster. Angela nudged me. I guessed I had missed my name.

"Present," I said, and everyone laughed.

"Yes, I can see that, Ms. Kelly. I asked if you were

up to running today." I nodded and ducked my head, my cheeks burning but it had nothing to do with the heat. I could smell the orange Gatorade coming off his breath from fifteen feet away. I inhaled again more deeply. Rubber from the turf track we were standing on, the smell of clean sweat, *my own*, and Angela's peach body mist invaded my nostrils. Another breath. I recognized the overwhelming flowery perfume coming from the cheering squad. It made my eyes water. I looked over at the group of boys stretching and getting ready to run. I identified Safeguard deodorant, like my uncle used, and spicy Doritos. Yuck! I was almost afraid to breathe again, but when I did, ah, fabric softener. It was *him*, Sebastian. His scent was like fresh laundry and a lightly fragranced soap. I could even smell the Mentos he was chewing. *Mmmm, minty fresh.* I wished I was standing closer to him. He smelled seriously good. I shook my head. This was impossible. *How could I smell that from all the way over here?*

Coach Vinnie blew his whistle. I threw my hands up over my ears and shut my eyes. The noise was so loud it was deafening. It took me a minute to shake it off. When I looked up the class was already running. As usual, Sebastian led the pack. I stayed behind with Angela. We all started running in a slow meandering sort of way. Angela struggled to keep up and the cheer-leaders made excuses to stop and stretch before jogging daintily in place. As I moved one foot in front of the other I started feeling a little better. Then I felt *a lot* better. I was actually having fun, *in gym class*! I moved faster. I felt so free. Light and strong. I had never experienced anything like it in my life. I could forget everything in those minutes. My brat of a cousin and her friends, my nagging aunt, the chores waiting for me at home, everything was gone. The only thing that existed was the pounding of my feet on the track and the wind on my face. In that moment, I felt like I was flying.

Far too soon Coach Vinnie blew his whistle and signaled everyone to stop. I turned around, my hands clasped over my sensitive ears. That whistle was way too loud. When I looked the entire class was stopped. A few mouths hung open, and a couple of dirty looks were thrown my way. Sebastian was doubled over, breathing heavily and a good twenty feet behind me. I had blown right past him, and I hadn't even noticed. I felt eyes on me, heard the whispers. *Oh crap!* There I was, in the spotlight again, something I really hated. I looked down, tried to block them out.

"Kelly, Kelly!" Coach shouted and ran to catch up with me. He wheezed a little before speaking again.

"You been working out? Whoa, I never seen anything like it. Hey, I tell you what, how about trying out for the girl's varsity team? We may need you at our game this Saturday," he stood there looking at his chart and the stopwatch in his hands, excitement in his beady little eyes. The rest of the class stayed back except for Angela. I didn't know what happened. Julianna shot me a dirty look from the back of the crowd and Angela handed me a bottle of water.

"So that was some run! Why didn't you tell me you'd been working out? OMG don't look yet."

"What?" I had no idea what she was talking about, but that was how half our conversations went. She tended to go from one topic to another without pause or breath. Maybe that's why we got along. She talked and I listened.

"Here he comes! OMG! Okay now, look!" She gestured behind me and I turned nearly colliding with Sebastian.

"Grazi, right?" I nodded and stared at the perfect boy standing right in front of me, my mouth open. "That was some run, maybe you could show me your secrets after school sometime?" His crooked grin was like a punch to the stomach. I couldn't believe the school star was actually speaking to me. He waited expectantly, and I realized I had yet to answer him.

"Um sure," I said but not before Julianna could chime in. I didn't even see her walk over, captivated as I was.

"Oh, she can't Sebby, she has to do chores and stuff after school. But I'd be happy to jog with you before cheering practice starts." She steered him away, hanging on his arm as if he was her property. I narrowed my eyes.

"Hey Sebastian," I called after him. He turned around. His warm brown eyes focused on me. "I'll see you tomorrow at the track, 3 o'clock."

Angry as I was at Julianna it took me a minute before I noticed I had just accepted a sort of date with Sebastian. I couldn't believe it. One flash of his smile and I completely forgot about my lightning fast run.

"So, Grazi, how did you get so fast?" Angela and I headed towards the lockers slowly. We wanted the cheerleaders gone before we got in there.

"Um, I don't know. I got some extra sleep, the other night and my Nonna makes me this super antioxidant rich iced tea all the time. Maybe it's making me stronger or faster or something." I shrugged thinking about it. I didn't really notice anything different except for the fact that I had been enjoying myself until coach blew his whistle and I had flown by everyone. I mean, yes, my sense of hearing and smell seemed to have improved. Sight as well, I didn't squint to look at the board anymore and I never got headaches anymore when I stayed up late reading. My new physical condition led to my sort of date to jog after school with Sebby De La Cruz, so I wasn't going to question it. It was all good, maybe even great. Then the bodies started piling up.

4

"Maria, you see this? On the news? Two animal attacks at the park behind the middle school in Dover. Oh, this poor boy!" I had just finished loading the dishwasher, and I looked over Nonna's shoulder at the newspaper article she was reading. There was a picture of a young boy, eleven or twelve. It was a school photo, he wore glasses and had curly brown hair. His body was found ravaged and bloody after he was attacked by what local police officers believed to be a rabid wild animal. I didn't recognize him, but I felt bad. There was another photo of his parents, his mother caught in an agonized scream and his father moving to catch her as she fell. What a horrible picture to put in the newspaper! Putting someone's raw, unfiltered grief on display to sell papers was despicable. Well, I thought so anyway.

"You see another, look! The poor man. This other was a vagrant, they found him by the lake. *Madonna mia*! You be careful when you go jogging, *capisce*? Animal control says it's a bear or maybe a dog with the rabies. Say a prayer to the Blessed Virgin to watch over you, *si*? Now, come here, sit and have some cocoa with me."

"Nonna, it's too hot out for cocoa. I'm fine, really."

"Cocoa is good anytime, come on, now I put the whipped cream, *si*! It's very nice."

"Sure, Nonna," I smiled and sat down at the kitchen table and waited as she poured me a mug of steaming hot cocoa. She topped it off with a generous dollop of freshly whipped cream. I inhaled deeply expecting sweetness, but I could smell something was off. I looked at my grandmother, her gray curls frizzy in the humid air, she wore a soft pink short sleeved shirt and white shorts, slippers on her feet. She looked at me expectantly. I didn't want to hurt her feelings I took a sip. *Yuck!* Bitter. I managed to swallow and smile without throwing up all over the table.

"So, Maria, how is school? This boyfriend, you bring him here to meet me."

"Nonna he's just a friend."

"Yes, well that is good too. You need to be a good girl and study. No time for boyfriends, *si*? Drink your cocoa, come on."

"I'll take it to my room, Nonna. We have to bring in the harvest tomorrow before everything burns up outside in this heat and I need my sleep. Goodnight." I kissed her head and headed to my room. Technically I wasn't lying to her. I did bring my bitter cocoa to my room. I just didn't drink it.

That night the temperature held at 85 degrees. Not hot for noon, but for a fall night it was unbearable. I walked to my large bedroom window and opened the pale, yellow curtains. The moon was bright and full. A large golden disc so close I could touch it. It *called* to me. Tempted me. I wanted to run. I wanted to be free. Free from everything. I was fast and strong, wasn't I? Stronger than I could ever dream.

I felt powerful and fearless. I opened the window all the while staring at the moon. Dry, hot air greeted me. I could feel beads of sweat forming on my head and down my spine. My breathing increased. My stomach cramped. I crouched down clutching my abdomen. I must have knocked my mug onto the polished wood floor because I could smell the bitter cocoa filling my lungs. It hurt to breathe. I remember crying out and swatting at the stink of it. Soon afterwards I heard footsteps and my door swung open. It was that new priest, Fr. Gallagher, and my grandmother. They were arguing. I heard the priest's Irish accent as he spoke in clipped sentences.

"Did you give her the *Aconitum*?"

"Yes, I put it in her tea all month and the cocoa tonight too."

"But did she drink it?"

"She said so, *si*!"

"But you didn't watch her drink it. Look there, it's all over the floor! You've kept her in the dark too long, Rosa. The girl should have been told."

"I have watched her and protected her. I didn't know we had so little time. Maria, *bambina mia,* look at me it's going to be okay, just breathe!"

"The signs have been there all along! You chose not to know! Damn it, Rosa, if she changes now, we won't be able to control her!"

"It is not your place, Sean! I will make her drink more cocoa. She will not change!"

"Get back, Rosa! There is no time!"

"You change too, *si*, and watch her! God, please save my granddaughter!"

"No, I, I can't. I drank it too. I am too weakened. Just get the length of *Gleipnir* from my bag!"

I could barely make out their words. I didn't understand what they meant, but I knew one thing. This priest was disrespecting my Nonna, and I wasn't having that. I lunged across the room and pushed him away from her. And yes, I think I *growled* too.

"Maria! No! Stop!"

Fr. Gallagher crashed into the shelf and fell to the floor. He staggered to his feet and I circled him. I breathed in the acrid stench of his fear. It excited me and it scared me. *What was happening?* Another cramp and I was back on the floor. I could hear my bones cracking. *My God, was I dying?* I started to pray in my mind in earnest. *Our Father, Who Art in Heaven, Hallowed Be Thy Name...* And then there was no pain. I opened my eyes.

My vision was somehow askew. I tried to stand. Something was off. I fell down! Scared. Angry. Confused. I cried out and heard something else. Not my voice! Panic welled up in my chest. I was panting. Tearing at my furniture, my bedspread with, not my hands. Were they *claws*? I howled in panic then something large with shaggy blonde fur hit me from the side. Long teeth nipped at me, and I turned to defend myself. I remember biting and growling. Then something soft and long landed around my throat, someone pulled it tight, and then everything went black.

The next day I woke up on top of my covers. I was dressed in an old nightgown. I didn't remember changing my clothing. Were these my old teddy bear sheets? Where did they come from? I reached around my throat, there was nothing there. I could have sworn something was around my neck during the night. My room was clean and smelled good, like clean linen air freshener. No spilled cocoa on the floor or shards of my broken mug. My curtains were closed. Everything seemed *normal*. I rubbed my eyes and my stomach grumbled loudly. I headed to the bathroom.

"What the heck!" My normal dull brown hair was hanging down my back in a tangle. That was not unusual. What was unusual was the brilliant streak of pale gold that shot down the front of my hair. An entire strip of hair about an inch and half thick, from root to tip, completely golden. My hand trembled as I reached up to touch it. Nope, it didn't come off. Definitely part of my hair. But how? I brushed my teeth hurriedly and washed my face with glycerin soap and ice-cold water. I quickly pulled on a pair of drawstring shorts and a t-shirt. I was super hungry and I needed some answers. I needed Nonna.

Downstairs the house was quiet. I looked around the kitchen. The clock on the microwave glowed a sickly green. It was past noon. Saturday. The girls would be shopping with their mother. Uncle Vito would be at his greenhouse and Nonna? Where was she? I opened the fridge and started picking on leftovers. My stomach was really growling now, and I shoved food in my mouth without even looking. I heard a creek in the floorboards. Fr. Gallagher was standing there. He leaned against the doorframe. In a pair of faded jeans, beat up hiking boots, and a black t-shirt. Not usual garb for a priest. A bandage was wrapped around his left forearm.

"We need to talk, *inion dearthar*."

"What are *you* doing here?"

"Like I said, we need to talk."

"Were you in my room last night?" Shivers ran up and down my spine as I stared at the unfamiliar man in my kitchen.

"Where's Nonna? What happened last night?" I looked down at the cold food in my hand and was disgusted by what I had inhaled in the last two minutes. "Oh my God, is this *salmon*? I hate salmon!" I covered the bowl I was eating from and thrust it back into the fridge.

"Your body is craving protein. Salmon is an excellent choice, *inion dearthar*. Your grandmother has given me permission to speak with you, Maria Graziana. Come now and sit down."

"What's an *inion dearthar*?" Something was wrong. I didn't know why, but this man put my hackles up.

"I've got things to tell you."

"I don't mean to be rude, Father, but it's a little creepy you wanting to speak with me alone."

"Don't you want to know about your father, Grazi?"

"My father! Did you know him?"

"Yes, I knew your father. Patrick was my older brother by three years."

"You're my uncle? I have an uncle?"

"You've got two uncles on your da's side. Michael is back in Ireland. It's complicated."

"Why haven't you come before this?"

"Your grandmother didn't want you to get to close to us if there was no need."

"Why would she do that? Why would she not want me to know about you?"

"Maria, you must try to keep your head. We don't have much time. The first battle is on St. Lucy's Eve, and you must be ready."

"What the hell are you talking about?"

"That is what I am talking about. *Hell*. And demons trying to claw their way out of the pit and into our world."

"Okay, I'm going to call the police now, you just stay there." Before I moved he walked over to me and put his hand on my arm, his voice was firm but not unkind.

"We fight them, Maria. We are *Werewolves*, the Hounds of God. I am currently the pack Beta, and I have come to train you, *inion dearthar*."

I stared at the man before me. I saw blue eyes, like the ones that shone from the wedding picture of my parents that I kept in my room. The curve of his cheek, the wave in his gray streaked blonde hair, were they familiar too? I couldn't tell. His accent wasn't thick, but I could hear the Irish lilt coming through loud and clear. He smelled like peppermint and rosemary. I tried to focus on what he was saying. Hounds of God? *What the fudge?* Was he crazy? The absolute belief he had in his words rang clear to me through his body language. I could tell he believed it.

"Can I call you, Grazi? I hear that's your nickname."

"Sure." I waited as he picked a chair from our table and sat down. I sat across from him. He looked at me directly and I met his gaze. He laughed and tilted his head, averting his eyes. Something in me recognized this as right and proper.

"Your father was first in line to become pack alpha,

after your grandfather, Rolf. Our family goes back generations with the Hounds. We are *servants* if you will, of the Holy Mother Church in Rome."

"What if I don't want to be a servant?"

"Our family is bound by a secret pact. So, Grazi, it's not really a choice. You're a Hound by blood and we've neglected your training for too long. We've got some serious work to do, you and I. The witches, have been preparing unchecked for too long and it's up to us to stop them."

"Werewolves? Secret Pacts? Witches? I think someone needs a nap." I attempted to shake off what he was saying with a bad attempt at humor, but his words didn't shock me as they should have.

"I'll tell you more as you train. Do we have a deal?"

"Tell me now."

"Where would I begin? There is so much you don't know. Come meet me in the basement of the Church on campus. I've set up a training room there. Come by after classes end and I'll tell you everything you want to know in time."

That was how my long-lost Uncle Sean Gallagher Kelly, aka Fr. Gallagher, introduced me to my fate. Like my father before me, I, Maria Graziana Kelly, am a Werewolf.

5

My work in the school library became the only time I could really clear my head. Ms. Vorax didn't seem to mind the quiet and I preferred it. She seemed preoccupied and she looked thinner than ever by Friday afternoon. I noticed her reading that big leather book again though she tried to keep it hidden underneath her desk. I wondered if I would find any information on Werewolves in it.

"Excuse me, Grazi? I'm going head off to the ladies' room for a minute, okay? You can cover things in here till I get back." She excused herself and I waited for her to exit the room then I took my chance. I carefully picked up the book from where she had put it under the desk and skimmed the index. It was written in English, but it was old. As in *ye really olde booke.* There were detailed illustrations covering the pages. Beautiful really, but I had no time to admire the artwork. I came across a page depicting a Wolf-man on two legs. It was an ugly creature and in his arms, was the body of a ravaged woman. Underneath it said, "*Ye accursed wulfman or wyrwulf dines on the weak and fragile. Women and children, the Devil's owne prefers to indulge in the bloode of ye innocents. Some villages sacrifice the ill or bastard borne to appease the beasts. Forsaken by God, ye wulfman is the Devil's own pet. He obeys his master's call and is a true hellhound.*" I stared in horror at the image. Saliva dripped from huge elongated fangs. It had a small female child in its arms with huge slash marks across her small chest. It was horrible. I had seconds to contemplate what I just read. I could hear Ms. Vorax's footsteps approaching. Before she could turn the doorknob to the library I had replaced the book and had gone back to restacking a series of old Encyclopedias in the research section. Funny books really, but I guess that's what people used before *Google.*

"Ms. Vorax, I wanted to ask you how your research is coming along?" I asked her as she approached her desk. She looked around as if she could tell something was amiss. I hated it when teachers did that.

"Oh, um, very good, Maria, thanks. So how are your classes? I hear you are quite the student."

"They're fine, thanks."

"I also hear there is a big dance coming up."

"Yeah, it's the Annual Harvest Dance."

"So, are you going to go with Mr. De La Cruz? You guys have been hanging around together a lot."

"Oh, we're just friends. You know, we jog together, that's it really." Spending time with Sebastian on the track a couple of times a week was probably the most I'd ever been with a boy. My heart sped up at the thought of going to the ball with him. I shook my head, there was no way he'd ever ask me. Who was I kidding?

"You know you could ask him," Ms. Vorax said with a sly smile. "Stranger things have happened, Maria." I smiled back, *she really had no idea.*

"Oops, there's the bell. Enjoy your lunch."

"Thanks. You too, Ms. Vorax."

"Oh, I will," she said and smiled again.

I was grateful to leave the library. It was stifling in the relentless heat. The air was stale and it smelled like mold or maybe a dead mouse or something. My conversation with Ms. Vorax got my mind working. Maybe I *could* ask Sebastian to the ball? I grabbed a tray from the stand and picked up a smoked turkey on rye with lettuce and tomato and a carton of milk.

I sat outside in the quad, away from the crowded cafeteria. Angela was nowhere in sight and I didn't want to sit inside alone. I sat under an oak tree near the track, it was the only place that offered a little shade that wasn't occupied. I no sooner bit into my sandwich than Sebastian plunked down next to me in all his glory. His hair was casually mussed and true to form he had no books. He *never* seemed to carry any books with him. He playfully bumped my shoulder and took a deep breath while turning his face up to the sun. He seemed happy. Sebastian had a relaxed air about him like he was exactly where he wanted to be and he knew everyone was glad he was there too. The kind of guy every girl at school dreamed about, but not conceited or stuck up. The polar opposite. He made *you* feel valued and important. It was a gift.

"Hey, Grazi! What's goin' on?" He never said much, even when we jogged. He seemed to appreciate my desire for silence. I loved to run now and he seemed to like it too. He said I challenged him to do his best. He had no idea that by now I could run circles around him.

"Hey, um, I'm good. Just grabbing lunch." I tried to swallow the bite I had taken without choking, shocked as I was by this unexpected visit. He kept looking at me from under his dark lashes and I could feel my heart speed up.

"Yeah, I see that." He smiled and brushed a crumb off my lip and I was shocked by the gesture. He never moved to touch me before.

"So, I think all our work has been paying off. I was two minutes ahead of everyone at practice this morning."

"Great! Um, you guys practice in the morning?"

"Yeah, you know, so it's not so hot. From 6:00-7:30 most mornings."

"Oh. Cool."

"Yeah."

"So,"

"So..."

He smiled and I looked down. We sat together for a while after that. Not really looking at each other, but not looking away either. He reached his long-tanned fingers over the cool shaded grass. I could feel it nearing mine and my own fingers strained towards him. I'm not sure who moved first, but we *touched*. Our hands wove themselves together, I could feel his pulse. Soon my heartbeat with his. He smelled wonderful, like fresh laundry and sunshine. I smiled and his hand squeezed mine.

"Will you come to the track today?" His voice was so nice, not too deep like some boys but not girly either. He had a tinge of pink across his cheeks like he got when we went running. My heart continued to thud in my chest.

"Yeah sure, after my, um, lessons. Five o'clock?"

"Good. I'll see you then." Another squeeze and he sprinted away as the bell signaling next period rang. I sat there in a stupor looking at my hand. Had Sebastian really just sat by me in the quad during lunch? Where everyone could see? I smiled in wonder until one of the cheerleaders walked by and knocked my tray over.

"Ooops. You'll clean that, won't you?" Expectedly, I was late to my next class.

"Again!" Fr. Gallagher, *aka Uncle Sean*, thrust a broom handle at me. I blocked and moved. My reflexes quicker than ever. I had no formal training in martial arts or fighting, but I was fast and I was strong. My body seemed to know what to do before my mind did. The sound of wood breaking brought my attention up. I had crushed the handle of the broom in my hand. I dropped the broken bits of wood and somersaulted to a position by the door. I dropped into a crouch and swung my leg out catching my uncle behind the knee. He fell to the floor with a thud and I had him pinned.

"That's a good move there, girl. You're getting stronger."

I stood up and reached for my bottle of water. I took a long drink and wiped the sweat from my brow with the hem of my shirt. He was right. I felt strong. Along with the gold streak in my hair, it seemed I was gaining muscle. I was always on the thin side, but now my body was toned, sleek and muscular. My legs had curves in them now and my abs were pretty awesome if I did say so myself. Heck, I even had a bit of a chest developing. I allowed myself to get distracted and wound up on the cold hard wood floor. My uncle's foot hovered just above my throat.

"Grazi, you must concentrate. Never let yourself be sidetracked in the middle of a fight. The full moon approaches and with it your change. I cannot teach you everything you need to know before then. You must try to focus. Learn control."

"I am concentrating, Fr. Gallagher. It's not easy. I'm just supposed to believe I'm a Werewolf and destined for some big battle. But I'm just a girl, a teenage girl. What can I do?" He extended his hand and I took it.

"My niece isn't just some teenage girl. Truly, you are so much more. You are important. And, uh, it wouldn't kill you to call me Uncle Sean, would it?"

"Yeah, okay." We continued sparring and working out. *Uncle Sean* set up a treadmill for me and I ran ten miles so quickly I thought I broke the thing. I much preferred running outdoors, but it was almost impossible for me to go full speed without drawing attention to myself. He handed me a bottle of protein water and my towel. I drank greedily and wiped the sweat from my brow, grateful for the ponytail that held my long hair off of my neck.

"Okay, we spent two hours working out, now you answer a question. That was the deal."

"Aye."

"How can this be real? How can I be a Werewolf?" He walked over to a pile of books set up on a makeshift desk on the other side of our training room. He looked barely disheveled. Two strenuous hours sparring and he hardly broke a sweat.

"Are you a Werewolf, too?"

He paused in our training room in the basement of the Church right on the school grounds. No one knew Fr. Gallagher was my uncle, we decided to keep that a secret. But still it wouldn't be unusual to see a student head over to the Church after classes. I watched as my uncle fingered a bent page. Before we began our physical training, we had gone over some basics of being a Werewolf. For example, all Wolves have different individual areas of strength, like some Wolves have like better hearing than others, but for the most part we all had superior hearing and olfactory senses. Werewolves healed quickly, were faster and stronger than regular people and, my personal favorite, got real hairy at each full moon.

"I told you already I am Beta of the Pack Greyback. That means second in charge. Rolf, your grandfather, is Alpha and Michael is a soldier. The Hounds of God is a vast army of various packs across Europe. We are indeed all Werewolves. Just not like you."

"What makes me so different? And how many Werewolves are there?"

"In our pack, there are over a hundred, but we are a larger pack."

"You said Europe. What about here?"

"As of yet, there are no American packs officially affiliated with the Hounds of God. It's complicated. There are political reasons, most likely uninteresting to you." I didn't disagree with him so I waited for him to continue.

"How am I different, Uncle Sean?"

"I don't know, Grazi, but we need to find out. Have you been following the news?"

"You mean the animal attacks?"

"Yes," I could feel his tension rolling off him in waves. "Started around two moons ago. Can you remember anything about it?"

"No, I-, I mean that was when I was sick at school…" Horror and apprehension. "You don't think that I-"

"We don't know, Grazi. We've not had a Wolf like you in a long time. There are no documented cases, no records. There are things we don't know."

"What do you mean a Wolf like me? What is different about me?"

"Well, your ancestors are Italian and Irish, and more-"

"More what? So, because I am Irish and Italian I'm some sort of mixed breed Wolf? WTH? This isn't the 19th century? Plenty of people have Irish and Italian descendants!"

"No, Grazi, I didn't mean that. Look, it is complicated."

"You keep saying that! Whatever I am, I would never hurt anyone!"

"But your Wolf *could*. Especially if you can't control her."

The horrible truth that rang in my uncle's words haunted me for the rest of the lesson. Apparently, I was some kind of secret big deal. I was not ready to believe what he and Nonna so readily accepted. Like, how could I be a *Werewolf*, like a *real Werewolf*? It was inconceivable! *Great, I sounded like the annoying guy in that princess movie. Oh boy!*

I knew I was changing, but I could not make the connection between the physical changes I was experiencing and the possibility that I was an actual Werewolf. I mean, how could they all expect me to make that leap from a little muscle gain? And the thought that *I* could have actually harmed a person? That man I knew from the convenience store, the homeless man, that little boy too? *Oh God, could it have been me?* I didn't want to believe it. I felt like I had to vomit just considering the possibility.

"Midwinter will be here sooner than you think, child, it is all connected. I must teach you to talk to your Wolf."

"But my Wolf is me? What do you want me to do, talk to myself?" I was exasperated at this point.

"Your Wolf is a part of you. Granted, she is a strong part, but she is separate too. Her heart is your heart, but her instincts are her own. She is designed to protect you. She doesn't think like you, and an untrained Werewolf is an animal at heart. That is why we undergo strict training from infancy, so that we may *know* our Wolves. You have yet to commune with her. It is vital you learn how.”

“What am I?” I could hear the despair in my voice. Was I some monster who took innocent lives? A ravaging animal?

“You are still you, Grazi. It is okay for you to need some time, child. It is a lot to take in.” I held my head in my hands as my uncle spoke. *A lot to take in?* That was a serious understatement.

“Let’s go over the reading assignment I gave you last night. Did you look up Peter Stump?”

“Yeah, Peter Stump was dubbed the *Werewolf of Bedburg*. So, what are you saying, he was an actual Werewolf? Does that mean I am capable of doing what he did too?”

“No, listen, what you must understand is that he committed horrible crimes, serial murders and cannibalism, and he blamed it on his lycanthropy. His Wolf followed *his* lead, Grazi. The truth is Peter Stump was a madman.”

“I’m sure plenty of people would think I’m nuts too if I told them I was a teenage Werewolf!”

“Regardless of him being a Werewolf, Peter Stump was a psychopath, Grazi. The point I’m trying to make is, he had no pack. He was untrained. The lunacy of the man infected the beast. He was uncontrollable."

"So, some pack controlling him would have been better?"

"Grazi, having pack means being a part of something bigger than yourself. Like a *family*, but so much more. Your pack understands you, cares for you, and protects you. It nurtures you. Teaches you. The Hounds of God are an elite group of packs within the Werewolf community bound by a covenant with the Almighty to protect society. What better back up to have than that?"

"So, it's some kind of cult?"

"No, we're not a cult! Are you daft, girl?"

"I'm sorry! It's just too much! So why was Stump executed if no one believed in Werewolves?"

"Actually, many people did believe him. At that time, there were many trials against those accused of being Werewolves. It was thought that Werewolves were evil and they worked for the forces of darkness."

"Darkness. So, what, like, my Wolf could be evil?"

"I sincerely doubt it, Grazi. *You* are not evil and your Wolf, well, she is bound to you, to your soul. If she were evil you'd have to be evil first. But a Wolf is an animal, a hunter. It is in the nature of the beast to hunt."

"Yeah, but if Werewolves were thought to be evil for hundreds of years there must be some truth to it. I mean rumors usually start with a bit of truth, right?"

"Let me try to explain it to you like this, Grazi. Human beings can be either good or evil. As can Werewolves. We, however, are employed by the Catholic Church to keep the people of Earth and their bounty out of the hands of demons."

"I've gone to Catholic school my whole life, *Father Gallagher*. I know just what the Church has done and it wasn't all great." I admit I was being catty and a little obnoxious. But hey, my life as I knew it was over. I think I had a right to be.

"True enough. The Church has had many ups and downs over the last two thousand years. Corruption, dishonesty, misuse of power. Countless crimes can be attributed to the Catholic Church going back to the first popes. But, the Hounds of God is a righteous group. We choose the path of righteousness and we *are* holy indeed, anointed by God. We wage war with the Devil's minions for the right to hold domain over the Earth. We are its protectors."

"The Devil, like *the Devil*?"

"Yes, there is only one Devil, and he is forever waging war with the Almighty. His minions here are many. They take many forms, do many bad things. The witches are his strongest servants. They use blood magic to create chaos and destruction. They are thieves. They are the bringers of plagues and famine. The murderers of innocence."

"How do we stop them?" I trembled with energy. My body hummed as I listened to my uncle talk about what we would face in the months to come. I felt scared. Terrified really but determined too.

"First, you must learn what you are. Tonight's homework I want you to read about Thiess of Kaltenbrun."

I left my lesson with Uncle Sean frustrated and confused. I hefted the huge leather-bound book he gave me and shook my head. *Jeez, ever heard of an e-book?* It smelled too, like dust and something else I couldn't quite identify. I stuck it in my backpack and slung it over my shoulder. I felt as if a huge weight had settled over me, and no, not just in my school bag. How could I keep all of the people on Earth safe? It was ridiculous. Unfair. Unbelievable!

6

I floated through the following day at school barely paying attention to any of my classes. It was all surreal to me. *How could I focus on Algebra when I'd be facing witches in the weeks to come?* I watched Sebastian make his way around the track after the last bell had rung. All of the mixed feelings I'd had since the previous night's lesson with Uncle Sean melted away. Replaced with awe and a little longing.

The sun was still fairly high, but it was cooling off to a steady seventy-eight degrees. Yeah, weird but I had my own personal weather center now and I could tell the weather right down to tenths of a degree, along with wind pressure. *I was such a weirdo.* Sebby was so blissfully unaware of how different we were and it made me want him all the more.

I sighed and looked around. I longed for the traditional oranges, reds and yellows of fall. The extreme heat and lack of rain had made this the dullest autumn I had ever witnessed in my lifetime. Hard, brittle leaves with no color fell from nearby trees, evergreens usually heavy with pinecones this time of year dropped heaps of dried out needles on the brown grass. Sebastian stopped to take a sip of his ever-present bottle of water. The sun highlighted his short dark hair throwing off streaks of amber as if he were aglow. He drank deeply, I watched his throat contract as he swallowed and my lips opened in response. His clean sweat assailed my nostrils and my heart sped up. He smelled good, healthy and alive. His heart thudded wildly in his chest from his run. I could hear it so clearly as if my head were pressed against his chest. I wished it was. Just then he noticed me and I jumped a little. I was embarrassed. I *had* been staring, but to be caught doing so. *Ugh, I'm such a dork!*

"Hey, you made it!" He jogged over and seemed actually happy to see me.

"Yeah, I'm sorry I'm late. I had stuff do it," Startled out of my temporary trance I walked towards him and missed a step. Balance and agility second nature now, I quickly righted myself, I set my backpack down next to where his was off to the side of the track.

"Let's get going then," Sebby started back down the lane, and I caught up to him easily. My uncle's voice played back over in my head. Rather unwelcomed, I should mention. All I wanted to do was concentrate on the cute boy I was jogging with. *How could I be one of the Hounds of God? Chosen to fight with the devil's minions?* A tiny squirrel rustled in the dead grass on my right. He was thin, there were meager pickings this harvest and he was suffering as well. As he scavenged for something to eat, to horde away for the coming winter, I locked my eyes on him and felt saliva fill my mouth. *Ew!* The poor thing retreated up a tree, I could hear its tiny heart beating rapidly. I shook my head. Wolves were hunters it made sense, but still. *Gross!*

I refocused on where I was and saw Sebastian. He breathed heavily, the veins in his neck popping out. I realized he was at his breaking point. I slowed my pace. I didn't want to embarrass him or damage our newly budding relationship. After all it was hardly a fair match. The rest of our run went by too fast. We stood by the bleachers drinking water and stretching. I could have run for miles more, but I tried to look winded.

"So, are you going to the Harvest Ball?" He looked right at me. His warm brown eyes focused on mine. I tried not to notice the swell of his muscles when his t-shirt pulled tight around his chest with every stretch and bend. He looked really amazing.

"Um, no, I don't think so." I ducked my head. How could I tell this beautiful boy I had never been to a dance? No one had ever asked me and I lacked the friends to go in a group. Last year I distinctly remembered hiding up in my room as Julianna took over the house getting ready. Nonna was at Mass, and I should have gone with her. Some sick part of myself wanted to stay home and witness my perfect cousin. Sure, she was a jerk, but she was *so pretty*. She wore the same color blue as her eyes, her mom had taken her to get her nails done and her hair in a cute up-do. I watched from the top of the stairs as Aunt Theresa gushed over her, snapped pictures and stuff like that. *Would my mom have been proud of me? Would she have taken me to get a mani-pedi and my hair done?* Those were things I'd never know. They didn't even notice me as I watched from the stairs. It sucked being invisible. *Yup, this year I was definitely going to Mass!*

"Oh, well, that's too bad because I wanted to know if you wanted to go. With me." He smiled at me. Open and friendly. Was he kidding? I waited a beat, but he just looked at me, his perfect eyebrows raised waiting for a response.

"Really? I mean yes. Yes, sure, I'll go."

"Great!" He linked hands with mine and grinned at me, his white teeth sparkling.

"That was a great run. I'll see you tomorrow, Grazi." He pulled me into his arms for a quick hug I thought, but then he kissed me. A sweet, soft kiss on my lips that left me too stunned for words. His cell phone chirped and he grabbed it from his pocket.

"My dad's here, I'll text you later. Bye." I could barely reply to his goodbye. I walked on air all the way to my bus stop. I soon realized I missed the last bus. *The heck with it.* I decided to run all the way home. I stuck to the woods behind the houses and roads, that way I could go faster than would be explainable. I reveled in the freedom of running through the trees.

My backpack weighed nothing at all, but maybe it was because I was stronger than ever before. I couldn't stop thinking about *him.* Sebastian filled my mind. Sweet, beautiful, Sebby with his dark hair and brilliant smile. *He kissed me! Me!* I could still feel his full soft lips pressed against mine. I could taste the raspberry-lime flavored water he had on his breath. I felt elated. I reached home much too soon. I jogged up the paved driveway to the door and was shocked to see Julianna waiting for me there.

"You! How could you do this?" She shrieked at me. Now, my cousin Julianna usually ignored me at home.

I was truly stunned that she was talking to me, well screaming at me, but I was in too good a mood to care. I shrugged past her. *Great. What did I do now?*

"You little bitch! You knew I wanted him! That's the only reason you're throwing yourself at him! Mom! Mom!" I set about depositing my school bag on the floor and taking off my sneakers on the bench in the foyer as she shouted for her mother. *Oh, even better, now my aunt would start in on me.*

"What? What happened now?" My Aunt Theresa came into the living room her hair in curlers and cream bleach smeared along her upper lip.

"*She* did it! She embarrassed me in front of all my friends! Everybody's talking about! Look at this post on Ur-Shotz!" Julianna was shaking with anger as she held up her cell and showed a picture of me and Sebby jogging. *So what? We jogged every day, I thought to myself.* "You little orphaned freak! She was sneaking around, mommy! With a boy! *My* potential boyfriend!"

"What are you talking about, Julianna? We were jogging." I was at a loss.

"Huh! Yeah right!"

"This is just like you, Maria. What do you have to say for yourself? Acting like that!" My aunt stood there, hands on her ever-widening hips, tapping her pink polished toes.

"Yeah, what did you give Sebby to make him ask you anyway? You do it with him behind the bleachers? You probably did it right there like an animal! You knew I was planning on going out with him and you tricked him into asking you out! You always want everything I have! My classes, my hair, my father's time, you want to be *me*!" She shoved me. She hardly moved me, but still. Before that point I thought the whole thing was pretty amusing and as things usually went with my cousin, of absolutely no importance to me. Julianna was used to getting everything she wanted. It must have really burned her that for once she envied me. However, after she put her hands on me I *so* did not care how she felt. My Wolf snarled in response to the physical threat.

"Do not touch me, Julianna." I said at what I totally considered a reasonable decibel.

"Maria Graziana, shame on you! Is this how you repay us for our kindness? You dishonor your family like a common tramp? It's just like you to stab your poor cousin in the back!" Aunt Theresa tried to rub her daughter's shoulders, but my cousin was on a real role. I trembled with anger at the venom in her perfect blue eyes. She poked me in the chest with her manicured finger and continued her rant.

"Lizette saw you guys on the track when she was leaving for her dance practice. Uh huh, so don't bother denying it! She posted that picture on Ur-Shotz so there is proof! Is that where you gave it up? You little slut! Just like your mom! You'll probably be knocked up before you graduate too!" She spat the insult in my face and went to shove me again. I felt the growl leave my throat and before I could stop myself I had Julianna up against the wall, my fingers wrapped around her skinny neck. The screams of my aunt barely registered. I didn't even feel the pounding of her fists on my back. Nonna brought me back to reality. I felt her strong hands on my shoulder as she said my full name in a gentle, yet firm voice, "Maria Graziana Kelly, put down your cousin right now."

"You're crazy! She's crazy! Vito, Vito!" My uncle came running and found his daughter gasping on the floor and his wife in hysterics.

"What is going on here?" He said still trying to swallow his last bite of dinner. *Mmm, smelled like fresh ham.*

"Your horrible niece! That is what is going on, Vito! I tell you I won't live here with her anymore! Not for one minute! She needs to go! Get out you little tramp!" She shook her finger at me and Uncle Vito covered his eyes and rubbed his head.

"*Basta!* That is enough! Theresa, you are a guest in *my* home, don't you forget that, si*gnora*! You act like a fool. You shame my son! Julianna stop your whimpering, you cry baby. You think I don't see. You think I don't know how you treat your poor cousin! *Disgraziata!* My own granddaughters!"

"She tried to choke me, Nonna!"

"And what did you do to her, ah? A little push a little shove, ah? I'm not so old I can't see, you know!"

"She's just your favorite!" My cousin whined then pretended to cry a little as her mother took her and wrapped her arms around her precious child.

"You are *both* my blood, both my granddaughters. This is enough now, *finito, si*!"

"Rosa, you are grossly unfair to Julianna," Aunt Theresa attempted to speak again, but Nonna glared at her and cut her off in a raised voice I had never heard her use.

"That is enough, Theresa! Bring your daughter to her room, get Rebecca out of here as well. Maria, go upstairs and wait for me."

I could not believe it. My grandmother had just told off my aunt and my cousin. If I hadn't recently been told I was a Werewolf and if the boy of my dreams hadn't just asked me out and given me my first kiss I think I might have been too shocked to move. It certainly was a month for revelations. My uncle stood silently and almost disgustedly at his wife and daughter. I looked from one face to another and decided my room was probably the best place for me right then.

"So, I hear you had an interesting evening last night," Uncle Sean said as he handed me a blindfold.

"Yeah well, that's putting it mildly." That Saturday morning was shockingly cold. It had dropped thirty degrees overnight. Yup, forty-five degrees and it was already noon. Almost unheard of in this part of the country, especially at this time of year. Usually, there was a ten to fifteen-degree shift in the weather, but this was ridiculous. I shivered in my long-sleeved t-shirt, clearly, I could have gone with sweats.

Whatever green was left outside from the intense heat was now frosted over. Farmers were in an uproar as prices plummeted and soared again. My uncle had to leave early that morning to clear fallen branches and weeds and to wrap fragile plants and trees in his various clients' yards. Luckily, we finished picking our own meager harvest the week before or it would have been frozen over. Now it was just a matter of clearing debris and setting up our garden for winter. I would help with that as I did every year.

"I know it is tempting to put that spoiled brat cousin of yours in her place, but you must resist. You could have hurt her."

"She called me a slut. She called my *mother* a slut!"

"You're not a slut, are you? And your mother was nothing of the sort. You know that don't you, Grazi?"

"I know and I'm sorry. I just *lost* it."

"Yes, I understand. But you cannot afford to lose it now, Grazi. Mean girls will always be mean, Grazi, it's their own insecurities that lead them to it. Try and forgive. Now put this on. We need to do a mind exercise."

"Great, first I get a 'turn the other cheek' lesson and now I'm supposed to be a Jedi."

"Ha ha ha. Just listen. Ok, make sure you cannot see. Good. Now I want you to think back to the night you first changed and tell me what you remember."

"I didn't feel well. I can't remember changing. Just cramps. Brief, intense pain. Lots of emotions."

"Like what? Were you able to think rationally?"

"I don't know what you mean. It was weird, but I was in there."

"Try and picture yourself. Your grandmother gave you cocoa. Did you drink any of it?"

"Yes, a sip in the kitchen. It tasted terrible."

"Hmm? Yes, for certain it did. It was the aconitum.

It is awful tasting especially to Wolves. Commonly called *Wolfsbane*. It stops the change when ingested. Well, usually, at any rate."

"I guess I didn't drink enough?"

"Yes, well that's the thing. Most of us that are left can't even attempt to change if we ingest the slightest drop. It weakens us considerably. Your grandmother put concentrated amounts of Aconitum extract in your tea and cocoa for weeks before the full moon. You should have went right to bed that night with one sip. Yet you managed to shift, and not into any half-beast. You were pure Wolf." I could not see my uncle but I could hear the awe in his voice. As if I were a mystery, a marvel even.

"Anyway, Grazi, I want you to try and *see* your Wolf."

I tried to do as he said, but I couldn't. How was a teenage girl from New Jersey supposed to deal with of this? Werewolves, witches... I didn't know.

"I can't, I'm sorry." I tore the blindfold off and I went to gather my things before he spoke again.

"Now don't get frustrated, girl. It'll take practice." I was ashamed of myself for not having better control, I knew he was my uncle, but he was also my teacher and I had never done so badly in any class. Granted these were not your typical classes.

"By the way, you have a new training partner coming on Monday."

"What do you mean?"

"His name is Ronan. He is a descendant of the original Hounds as are you. He was raised in the same small village in Ireland where your father and I were born. Mostly Werewolves there. And well, let's just say he would benefit from an education here in this country and you will benefit from him as well."

"Maria Kelly, front and center please. There you are young lady, boy you really sprouted over the summer! Now, let me introduce you to Ronan Madden, he's an exchange student. Fr. Gallagher is sponsoring him and we hoped you could, well, show him the ropes, you know." I stared at the giant boy in front of me as Sr. Diane spoke. Ronan was tall, well over six foot. He had short, strawberry blonde hair and a light dusting of freckles. His eyes were a piercing emerald green. He was really athletic looking. Must be a Werewolf thing. I mean my Uncle Sean was like, old, but he was in really good shape too. This boy in front of me looked like he worked out for a living. Long and lean, yet his musculature was very pronounced. The other girls were fanning themselves and getting an eyeful. Especially Julianna.

"Sr. Diane, I would be more than happy to show him around!"

"Yeah, we could all, like, give him a tour," giggled Lizette and Jennifer. *Clones!*

"Well, thank you, Julianna, but Fr. Gallagher assigned Ronan to Maria for now. Maybe you can sit with him at lunch? Isn't that nice!"

I ignored my cousin. It was the safer thing to do these days. What shocked me was Ronan did also. He barely glanced at her. He didn't speak. He just looked at me, recognition in his eyes. I thought I saw them *glow* for a minute. He tilted his head to the side and averted his eyes. *Was he submitting to me?* Uncle Sean had told me Werewolves were very conscious of body language. Posture, eye contact, a tilt of the head, standing, sitting; these things all had very specific meanings to Werewolves. I was sure Ronan was showing me he was submissive to me. I did not have any idea why he would do that, he definitely looked like he could kick my butt. I mean, he was gigantic. Muscular, tall, and he had obviously been raised a Werewolf his entire life. I'd been one for just a couple of weeks really. I still had no idea what was going to happen to me the next full moon. Maybe he was just being friendly? Hard to believe since he didn't even crack a smile.

"You are shorter and thinner than I expected," was all he said as we made our way down the hallway to the lockers. *Really? I am five-foot nine, hardly short! And I am thin but come on, what was he expecting a cow or just someone a little more top heavy? Like Lara Croft! Sexist pig!* He smirked as if he could read my thoughts, but I ignored him. I set him up with the locker directly under mine and waited as he grabbed some books. Then I took him to fill out some forms in the school office. Sr. Diane nodded at me when we left, but not before taking note of the length of my skirt. She gave me an approving nod and went on her way. *Great, I'm such a dork my school principal approves of my skirt length.*

"So, what's the plan, Princess?" I made no move to answer him as we walked down the hall together. I didn't know why but he irked me. I mean what was he? My babysitter?

"Okay then, no need to talk my head right off, princess," He smirked as he said it and I wanted to slap that expression right off his face. *I didn't have to talk to him if I didn't want to!* I knew I was acting like a big baby, but I couldn't seem to help it. So, I continued to ignore him. He followed me around the entire morning. At lunch, I watched as Ronan piled food onto his tray. He noticed the lone turkey sandwich on mine and added a salad, yogurt, carton of milk and an apple.

"Hey, I didn't want that stuff."

"Sure, you don't, princess. Leave it alone then if you don't want to eat it." He sat down next to me and started making his way through one of his four chili cheese dogs. "Mmm. Good." I cringed. I didn't eat hot dogs.

"You do know what's in hot dogs, right?"

"It's meat, right?" He took another monster bite.

"Yeah, um, barely. More like snouts and hooves." I watched as he devoured another one in two bites. He wore an expression of pure bliss. I shrugged and unwrapped my yogurt. It had real organic peaches, *yummy*.

"Hey, Grazi." Sebastian came and sat down on my other side with a smile. He kissed my cheek and unwrapped a turkey sandwich identical to mine. It made me idiotically happy that we liked the same things. Suddenly, I was embarrassed at the amount of food on my tray. Angela joined us too and I forgot my embarrassment for the time being.

"Hi, Grazi! Hi Sebby, and um Ronan, right? I'm Angela," She looked happy with all the male attention we had at our table and basked in Ronan's full-mouthed nod of recognition. *The slob!* Everything was cool for a bit, that was until the cheerleaders decided to come over.

"Hello boys! It's Ronan, right? I was wondering if you wouldn't be more comfortable with us over at the bigger table." Julianna leaned over the table deliberately shoving her bra enhanced boobs in his face. Disgusting really. Ronan didn't seem to mind. He smirked then must have remembered his babysitting post. He looked at me eyebrows raised and I shrugged as if to say go ahead.

"Be my guest." *Really, dude, go.* Julianna leaned into him again and he seemed momentarily hypnotized.

"You're certainly well fit, aren't ya." He cleared his throat and continued, wiping his hands on a napkin. *Thank heavens, he knew how to use one.* "Thanks much girls, but alas, I'm fine right here."

Julianna's smile dropped into a hard line. She shifted her attention and her boobs to Sebastian. His ears got a little pink and he fiddled with his napkin.

"So, Sebby, maybe you can sit with us. After all the Harvest Dance is coming up and since you are Junior class president I was wondering if you had any opinions on the decorations?" He answered her politely but managed to decline her invitation as well. That didn't seem to deter her. She sat next to him, waving her clones to have a seat. They all seemed to be sharing a single plate of sliced cucumbers and carrot sticks, no dip or dressing on the side. *For lunch, really?* I bit into my sandwich and sighed with gusto. Lizette shot me a dirty look. *LOL.* Julianna ignored me and sipped from her water bottle. She wound her perfect hair around her little manicured finger and asked Sebastian all sorts of questions about the dance. I tried to take another bite but couldn't manage it. Julianna sat there smiling her perfect teeth at everything Sebby said. *Ugh.* Life was so unfair sometimes.

"So, what's your deal?" I whispered to Ronan.

"My deal? I've made no deals nor bargains. I do not consort with witches or demons-,"

"Oh jeez, just chill with the demon talk," I looked over, but no one seemed to have heard us. Angela was busy mimicking Julianna with frequent hair flips and a huge vacant smile. Great now she was poking the dish of cucumbers. Sebastian was trying very hard to keep a straight face while my cousin monopolized him, hard with Angela's antics. My conversation with Ronan was so far unnoticed. *Thank goodness! Being overheard talking about witches and demons was not going to do me any favors!*

"You speak of deals and ask me to be silent? Is this

a joke to you, princess? I have been taught to fight this war since I was a pup. I am told *you* are to lead the battle, and you accuse me of *dealing* and then mock me when I deny it?"

"No mockery intended! No, really, I just mean that no one here knows any of this! No one would believe it if they did! Please, look we will train after classes with Uncle Sean. That is the only place we can discuss this. Please?"

"You plead with me? There is no need, princess. I shall do as you bid. I'm sorry for being cheeky." He looked embarrassed and averted his eyes even further. "The bell is ringing, let's go to our next lesson. I believe we have music."

The look in his eyes as he spoke, before he looked down, was so intense I couldn't reply. The second bell rang and Angela cleared my tray for me as I sat like an idiot. Ronan took my hand and pulled me up from chair. He handed me my school bag. Sebastian and Julianna were still talking. Well, *she* was talking. I noticed him trying to keep tabs on me and Ronan. Our voices dropped so low that had we not been Were-wolves I doubt we could have heard each other. As it was I had a hard time not hearing things I didn't want to. Like all the ultra-sweet *BS* Julianna was slinging at Sebastian!

"Oh, Sebby will you stop by my locker with me? I need your help carrying my designs for the dance over to Mrs. Bene's art room. Then we need to move the craft paper and supplies so we can start working on them," Julianna took his arm and led him away. He looked back at me as if to say he couldn't help it. Knowing my cousin, he really couldn't. I waved and mouthed, "See you later." He smiled at me like he knew he was forgiven.

"Great. That's settled then," Ronan took my arm again and dragged me down the aisle. I was getting awfully tired of being pushed and pulled by the guy. We went to the music room and he immediately sat down in front of the grand piano, pulling me next to him. The rest of the class was divided into groups, talking and fooling around. Some students were tuning their instruments. Music was usually a chaotic class. Half of the kids took it for an easy A, the rest were serious about ding the annual Christmas concert and spring musical.

"Ronan, I don't know how to play-"

"You don't? Oh well, it's good, I do then." His fingers began a dance across the black and white keys and what started as some warmup scales soon became a wonderful melody. Ronan looked around the room, but he wasn't seeing he was *listening*. Then he looked down his fingers flew gracefully over the keys. It was something classical I didn't recognize.

"Franz Liszt," he said answering my unspoken question. Then he transitioned from that to an old Cole Porter song I knew from my Nonna.

He sang the old fashioned, but sweet lyrics in a truly remarkable voice without embarrassment or shyness. Clearly, he was talented. He switched melodies again, this time going for, *I couldn't believe it*, it was one of my absolute favorite love songs. Students started swarming around us. Caught up in his voice as I was, I hardly even noticed. He crooned in his clear strong voice about love and longing. My heart thudded in my chest and I knew he could hear it. I could feel it in his green eyes. I leaned into him and closed my eyes, listening to the timbre of his voice and the unspoken messages passing between us. I almost forgot where we were. The class erupted in enthusiastic applause and cat calls. I snapped back to attention. My cheeks were hot and my breathing a little unsteady. Ms. McHafferty, the music teacher clapped wildly and approached the piano.

"Mr. Madden, how wonderful! Truly remarkable! How long have you played?" She asked Ronan a million questions. I tried to get up and walk away but he grabbed my hand and pulled me back down on the bench. *I was going to kill him.*

"My mother taught me to play, actually Miss. She teaches music back in Ireland." I noticed his accent came off real thick when he was charming the ladies. Apparently, it didn't matter whether they were sixteen or sixty.

"Well, you must play for our Christmas concert! Will you?"

"Surely, Miss."

"Great, Okay class, settle down!"

"What was that about?" I whispered as he dragged me to two chairs across the room.

"I don't know what you mean, princess."

"The serenading!"

"I was just singing a few songs. Didn't you think I carried the tune well?"

"You know you did. Why that song?"

"What? It's my favorite is all." He was telling the truth. It just seemed odd to me that we would both like that song. I wondered what Sebastian's favorite song was. I'd have to ask him. It was just too weird that Ronan and I would have stuff in common.

He spent the remainder of the day shadowing me. I was probably meaner to him than I should have been. It wasn't his fault I liked the Cure too. It wasn't his fault that a boy was finally interested in me. Not just any boy, but *the boy* and I had to be stuck with a giant red-headed watchdog. *Literally.*

I got about twenty text messages in between music and religion about whether or not I was going out with both Sebastian and Ronan and from people I didn't even know! One text, from Sebastian stood out.

Hey Grazi, a lot of people are saying some things about you and that guy you're showing around today. I know you better than that though. I just wanted to say don't let it get to you. I'll see you, later. XO

I felt so much better after that. I mean we weren't officially going out or anything, but still. I really liked him and I didn't want to ruin anything. *And he put a XO at the end of the text!* That was promising.

My relationship with Ronan had *nothing* to do with romance. I couldn't exactly tell Sebastian that he was here to show me how to be a Werewolf, but I could show him it was just a tutoring thing. *Yeah, that would work!* High school drama could be so ridiculous sometimes. I shut off my phone and prayed the day would be over soon.

7

"No, listen to me. Close your eyes. Picture the Wolf inside of you. She is part of you but separate too. Can you hear her?" Uncle Sean's voice was sharp. I could feel his tension, but what could I do? Trying to talk to my inner Wolf was a bit more complicated than he let on.

"Remember, once you commune with her you should be able to control her better." The idea of control was alien to me. I have never been in control of a single thing that has happened to me in my brief lifetime. My uncle's voice was soothing though and I closed my eyes. At first there was too much going on inside my mind. My parents' death, living with my cousins, being a freak, none of these things were in my control! I tried to focus on the moment and the day's events rushed through my mind like an internal instant replay.

Okay, Grazi, empty your mind like Uncle Sean said. I tried again and saw Sebastian on the track, tanned and gorgeous and smiling at me, then he was replaced by Ronan holding an apple out to me, then the dream with my mom tucking me in. It was like I was running down a tunnel of memories. *Empty your mind, Grazi! Concentrate!* I saw a brilliant flash of silver light. Then everything went black. All sound and light extinguished, as if I were in a vacuum. I saw a steady stream of white and silver light and I followed it. It was neither cold nor hot, it just *was*. I trusted it though and it led me to a large ball of swirling silver mists. *The moon.* An electric sort of hum settled over me. I saw a Wolf. My Wolf. Large, dark brown with a streak of platinum running down her muzzle. Her coat was thick and beautiful, her eyes a stunning shade of amber, like liquid gold. She grinned. *Yes, little one, I am here. I will protect you. I am yours.* Her message calmed me. It gave me a feeling of utter strength and purpose.

I gasped and opened my eyes. My uncle was crouched at my feet. Ronan was standing in the corner. He was in a military stance, you know the one, hands clasped behind his back, his legs shoulder width apart.

He turned his head towards me. "Is that your first time then? Talking to her?" He grinned, but still carefully avoided making eye contact.

"Yes! She, she, answered me. Spoke to me. I could see her." I wiped my face and felt moisture. *Had I cried?*

"Very good, Grazi. That was fast." Uncle Sean stood up and picked up another of his large dusty books. He ruffled his hair as he mumbled in what sounded like Latin to me.

"Is that weird? For me to speak to her so fast?" I felt buzzed, like I drank too much coffee. I wanted to go back, speak to her again. Maybe ask some questions.

"Took me nigh on a year to get my Wolf to answer my call. So yeah, I guess it is unusual then. But we didn't expect you to be typical, princess." Ronan shrugged, but seemed impressed.

"Why do you call me that?"

"Call you what?"

"Princess."

"What should I call you then?"

"You can call me Grazi, everyone does."

"Is that your real name?"

"It's Maria Graziana, Grazi is a nickname."

"If you request it of me, of course, I will call you by something else."

"Why 'of course'? You speak as if you have to obey me or something?"

"But I do-"

"Ronan! *Non dica verbum!*" Uncle Sean snapped his book closed and glared in our direction. I looked from him to Ronan. Ronan rubbed his head and shuffled his feet a little. His head still cocked to the side, glowing green eyes shifted downward.

"Aye, I've got to go, prince-, that is, *Maria*. I'll be seeing you." He nodded, *no* he bowed and left the room. His cheeks a little red. Could he be embarrassed? I didn't think so given his performance in music class, but I only just met him. Ronan would have to remain a mystery since he was rushing out of the room like his tail was on fire. *Ow, painful imagery!*

"Yes, that's a good idea. I'll see you later, Ronan. Don't you be getting up now, Grazi, we've got a bit more to do. A little field trip you might call it." Uncle Sean put his book back down and grabbed his keys. We left the workout room and he locked the door behind us. I followed him outside, past the school grounds to a stretch of woods. It was colder, our breath puffed out in clouds in front of us. I held my backpack on one shoulder and looked around us. The woods were comforting to me where before they would have seemed creepy at this time of day. The dry brittle grass crunched under our feet. First no rain and unbearable heat and now an almost frigid cold. The very earth itself at war with the weather. I watched as Uncle Sean knelt, he picked up a clump of grass.

"Here. Smell." I breathed deep and almost gagged.

"Well girl, what do you smell?" He grinned at me as he dropped the grass and wiped his hands on his jeans.

"It smells like pee, real strong pee," I couldn't believe I was saying that to my uncle. I rubbed my sensitive nose and he laughed.

"Aye, that is fox urine. There must be a den somewhere close this is fairly recent and strong. Now smell this."

Red fox. Close by, a female, she has a small litter. 2 or 3 pups. I recognized the voice in my head as her, my Wolf. It should have been strange to hear this voice inside of me, but it was pleasant. Comforting even. I could sense her longing. She wanted to run, to chase, but I was in charge. *Wasn't I?*

"Grazi? Come on, smell this one."

"What? No more pee, thank you very much." I wrinkled my nose and squinted at my uncle, he didn't seem to notice my momentary hiatus from our conversation.

"Grazi, it's not urine, I promise. I want you to tell

me if you can determine what kind of tree this is. You know other pups have had years to develop these skills." Exasperated my uncle held a leaf out to me.

"Yeah, but I thought the change only happened after puberty. So how far behind can I be? And it's a walnut tree by the way."

"Wow, you have some skills then."

"Not really, Uncle Vito has a landscaping business. I help him out now and then."

"That's good that you pay attention. Now, listen up. You have always had a better sense of smell, eyesight, and hearing than the average kid your age. You just didn't develop it. If you had grown up like most pups in the pack you would have been taken out camping since birth practically. And hiking, tracking, first aid, you know, the usual survival skills and such. Fighting, climbing, fishing, swimming. All of it."

"Hey, I can swim! Besides my skills have always been more mental than physical. Maybe I can outthink the bad guys?"

"Grazi, be serious. I'm trying to teach you something here."

"Fine," I muttered and knelt next to where my Uncle was crouched by a large Birch tree. He moved some dried dead leaves out of the way and showed me a small hole. After reaching inside he pulled out a chipmunk. The poor thing was trembling. My uncle grinned and his eyes glowed electric blue for a moment.

"'He cuts out rivers among the rocks, and His eye sees every precious thing.' Book of Job." I nodded my head.

"Yeah, I recognize it. I've read most of the Bible." *I mean hello, eleven years of Catholic school here.*

"Aye, you're okay, yes you are, little guy. No worries, I'm not hungry." He let the chipmunk go and as I listened I could hear him scamper back into his hole and dig as fast as his little claws could go. He *knew* what we were and he was afraid.

"It's nature's way, Grazi. God's way." I couldn't help it, I felt guilty. That we frightened the little guy. *Like we were monsters or something.*

We spent the next two hours walking in the woods behind the small campus of Sacred Heart Preparatory School. There are various hiking trails in Northwestern New Jersey, but the one we took was far off the regular beaten path. Uncle Sean insisted on it. We smelled things, listened for things, tracked small animals. I still couldn't get over the strange comfort and familiarity I found in my uncle's company. I mean you would think I'd had enough of relatives with my grandmother and uncle's family, but this was my *dad's* family. Here.

Now. Living, breathing and teaching me about things I never knew existed. Heck, a month ago I never knew he existed.

As we walked through a marshy area of woods, I felt bad for holding back. I hadn't told him about my ongoing communication with my Wolf. She spoke to me during our hike. She didn't exactly tell me things. It was more like she helped me use and trust in my senses. I don't know why I felt I should keep it quiet, but I did. Her strength and instincts seemed to seep into me from within.

We continued to walk for a while under the darkening skies. Woods became streets dotted with minivans and eventually we arrived at my home. It was very dark, but Wolves see well in the dark. I realized with a start that I had enjoyed myself. *Really* enjoyed myself. Uncle Sean declined my invitation to come inside. Probably for the best. Nonna spent most of her time glaring at him anyway. I think I surprised him, at least I know I surprised myself, when I threw my arms around him.

"Goodnight, Uncle Sean."

"Goodnight, *inion dearthar.*" He waited until I was inside before walking away. Back through the woods.

. . .

The next evening, I stood stretching and sipping my bottle of protein water after Sebastian, and I had our run. The hour passed by too quickly.

"Are you sure you don't need me to wait with you?" He asked while checking his cell.

"Nah, I'm okay. My Uncle Vito is on his way. You go ahead." He jogged over to his dad's car but not before giving me a quick kiss on the lips and squeezing my arm goodbye. We ran together almost every day now. And every day he would ask me if I needed a ride and offered to wait with me, but I always told him it was fine and my ride was on the way. The truth was I was so revved up after our run since I had to hold back when I ran with him that I had to run a few more laps by myself after he left. That night I had so much energy I thought I'd stay for a good long while. He smiled and waved goodbye from the car.

I looked around hoping to find an empty campus. Usually, we were the last to leave the outdoor facilities and I could finish my run-in peace. But that night my senses alerted me to someone watching me. I turned and saw Ronan walking out of the Rectory towards where I was standing. It hadn't occurred to me before, but I guessed that was where he was staying. The

Sacred Heart Rectory was connected to the Church. The Sacred Heart Prep building was relatively new, only sixty years old or so, but the Church and Rectory were not. Having been built at least fifty years before the school itself. The Rectory seemed old and a bit spooky to me. I had never been inside of it, but it made sense that Ronan would be staying with Uncle Sean. I wondered if Fr. Verrell had any idea who they really were.

"Hey there," He walked towards me in a pair of sweats, running sneakers, and a black t-shirt. "You finish playing around with your little boyfriend, then?"

"He's not my boyfriend-" Ronan cut me off with another of his infamous smirks.

"Yeah, well whatever he is, I know you'll be wanting a *real* run now. Come on, I found a great trail, no one will see us." Before I could ask why it mattered if anyone saw us Ronan took off behind the old Church. He darted behind some tall pines and I didn't waste any time. I followed him. We ran at a fairly brisk pace for a regular human up until we hit the woods. That was when the real fun happened. Ronan looked at me, his emerald green eyes alight with mischief, he smirked and then he really took off. I was startled into stopping for a minute. One minute he was there the next only his scent lingered. I quickly came to my senses and booked after him.

"Am I going too fast for you, princess?" I heard him laugh and call out to me. He was purposely goading me! *The rat!* But really, I loved it. I sped towards him, I had to be running about thirty miles per hour. Trees flew past me and I leapt over fallen branches and shrubs without a single stumble. I caught up to Ronan and he looked stunned to see me. That lasted all of a minute as his eyes narrowed and his determination *and* longer legs allowed him to gain the lead.

After a few more minutes of running at breakneck speed we slowed down. We stopped altogether at a nearby stream. Our breath puffed out from our mouths and we were both smiling. It was exhilarating. I had no idea I could run like that. It was amazing. I hardly felt winded, just excited really. Ronan walked over to the stream cupped his hands and took a long pull of the cool clear water.

"Wait a minute! You're not supposed to drink from a stream without boiling it first," I said horrified to think what might be in the water.

"Oh girl, you know nothing, do you? Here smell," he held out his hands to me and I smelled nothing unusual.

"If there were something in there that was harmful we'd smell it. You're a *Werewolf*, Maria. There's not much that can hurt you. No little bug in the water can make you sick. We've got supercharged immune systems. Think on it. When was the last time you were sick, and I mean really sick, not from the *Change*."

"I guess not since I was ten or eleven. So, what do you mean? I won't catch a cold or anything?"

"No, you won't catch a cold or anything. At least not by conventional means. I mean we are not invincible. We get old, though not at the same rate as humans, and we do die, but more often in battle than not. We can be cursed or bewitched, we can be hurt by demons, but drinking a little water from a stream can't hurt us."

I only half listened to what he was saying. The Irish lilt in his voice was mesmerizing and somewhat familiar. *My dad had talked like that.* I walked over to where he was crouched and smelled the water in his hands that he held out to me. I leaned in and took a drink. It tasted marvelous, but the intimacy was unexpected. He touched my neck and I pulled back. I smiled to break the awkwardness and leaned down to the water. I drank directly from the stream until I was full. I felt his eyes on me as I took long pulls from the cool, refreshing water.

"What?"

"Nothing. So, what are you and your boyfriend doing on that track every day?"

"He's not my boyfriend. And what do you care? Are you watching us?"

"Yeah, well you'll never get a proper work out with *him*, now will you?"

"I don't jog with him for a *proper* workout, besides I get that at Uncle Sean's."

"Then he *is* your boyfriend, why not just admit it?"

"He's not my boyfriend, okay?"

"Whatever, princess. You ready then?" We didn't bother stretching and ran back in tension filled silence. What was Ronan's problem anyway? Sebastian was a friend. Yes, he was extremely cute and yes, I was crushing on him a bit, but still, that was private. I certainly didn't want to discuss him with Ronan. What gave him the right to ask me questions like that? And what was with the princess crap again? *Ugh.*

"So how was your run?" Uncle Sean was waiting for us when we got back.

"Fine." We said in unison.

"You need a lift home then? Fr. Verrell said we could use his car."

"I'll drive her," Ronan said with a smirk as he caught the keys Uncle Sean tossed his way. I didn't understand that smirk until I got behind the wheel with him. Werewolves are capable of many things, but apparently driving wasn't one of them. You've heard of the term *speed demon*? That was Ronan. I don't think he drove under sixty, even on side streets. He had some heavy metal station cranked all the way up and wailed along with it as he drove. A few minutes later and we came to a furious stop in front of my house. I leapt out of the car and slammed the door. *I was so gonna get him back for this.*

"Well that was grand, wasn't it! Beauty of a car!" Ronan caressed the vintage Mustang's steering wheel. Fr. Verrell had a certain penchant for old Mustangs. This was his pride and joy.

"Are you crazy?"

"No worries, princess. I'll see you tomorrow." He took off at breakneck speed and I stood there with mixed emotions. I mean he was infuriating. Cute, but infuriating! Wait a second, Ronan wasn't cute! *Sebastian* was cute, Ronan was a jerk! *Get it together, Grazi!* I stormed into the house, angry at myself for my conflicting emotions.

I mean why did I insist on telling him that Sebastian wasn't my boyfriend? Especially when that is exactly what I wanted Sebastian to be? I mean who cares what Ronan thinks? I took off my sweatshirt and my sneakers in the small mudroom in the front of the house. My stomach growled immediately as the enticing aroma of roasted turkey breast and sweet potatoes greeted me. I headed for the kitchen hoping to find Nonna. I could use a little TLC and knew she'd be there with open arms. Only, she wasn't.

A lone plate of food, covered in aluminum foil, sat on the stove. My name was on a little pink sticky note stuck right on top. I looked for Nonna but couldn't find her. I took the plate up to my room. It was the first time I had ever eaten alone in my room since, well since ever. I *always* ate with Nonna. For the first time since my parents died I felt truly alone.

The days sped into one another. Halloween came and went in a flash. With the temperature drop, the approach of the Harvest Dance, and my recent communication with the beast that was me, and the absence of the only parent I ever knew I was a little bit stressed. Okay, *a lot* stressed. It was a lot to take in and I like to think I did an okay job of it. I went from being pretty much an invisible teenager to a teenage Werewolf in a matter of weeks. It sounded like a bad movie plot. I had so many questions. Like why did Ronan call me princess and claim I was to lead them in battle? He had to be kidding, right? I wondered if maybe I could find out more from him.

I wanted to ask him so many questions, but I didn't want to argue and after our little confrontation I felt *weird*. On top of that I wasn't getting any sleep. The dreams about my mom were happening almost nightly. It always ended the same. Her screaming for me to run. I had no idea what it meant, but it left me uneasy.

I walked into the cafeteria after finishing a pop quiz in Mr. Gundy's history class. I found European history interesting so I always read ahead and did research on my own. A good thing too. He tended to stray from basic facts like, 'What year was the Battle of Waterloo?' (1815 for those of you interested) to more philosophical questions like 'Was Napoléon Bonaparte a classic egomaniac or did he actually benefit the French? Please give examples.' I answered that though Napoléon was a genius at war strategy he seemed to be governed by an extremely overinflated notion of himself thereby causing him to dismiss democracy and crown himself emperor. I went on to discuss the highs and lows of his political career for two more pages, like his positive changes to the French civil code allowing for government positions to be held based on merit and not birth. Other students, like Ronan, simply stated "The brass *cojones* on that guy were admirable egomaniac or not." *SMH*. The guy was exasperating.

Ronan not Bonaparte, though if I thought about it, him too.

As I reached the food line I noticed the school was crawling with cops and just about the entire student body was crammed into the cafeteria. What the heck was going on? I decided to utilize my Werewolf hearing and picked up on a conversation on the other end of the room while I scooped up a protein bar and some yogurt. I was hungry almost constantly and small snacks packed with protein helped curb it a bit.

"Dude, Reggie found a dead body! For realz! He was looking to light up under the soccer bleachers and he like tripped. Right over the dead dude's foot! Yup, it was still inside its shoe! The same kicks we all wear! He puked all over the place, then ran screaming to the office. Idiot still had his cig in his hand!"

I listened to bits and pieces of conversations throughout the room and picked up on more the same thing. Dead body in the soccer field. A student. *Holy crap!* I said a quick prayer to the Virgin Mother and almost bumped into another kid. My yogurt wobbled on the tray, but I quickly righted it. Some students were crying, others were treating it with a sense of detachment like it was no different than any other piece of gossip.

Sr. Diane was making plans to gather us to

assembly the period after lunch to tell us what was going on. I could hear her in the hallway speaking to the police and the vice principal, Mr. Dennis. Unfortunately gossip and texting travelled faster than she did. Even the dimmest student had to figure it was something important given the amount of police activity outside. Most of the students were trying to guess the identity of the body. Compared to public schools, our high school was relatively small and most absences were easily noted. I noticed some of the teachers walking the cafeteria, asking students if they were okay. Some understandably took the opportunity to call their parents and go home. I just stood and watched, waiting to hear more until I sensed someone behind me.

Ronan. He had a scent uniquely his own. Cut grass, spicy cinnamon, and the outdoors, like he just took a walk in the woods. I could smell his Wolf too, he smelled like musk and forest. *Old, enchanted forest.* I closed my eyes for a second and breathed him in. I was startled as I realized I could *see* him as well. Large with massive forepaws and beautiful reddish tinted fur.

Yes. He is strong. Good too. He will help. It was my Wolf again. How do I talk to you? *You just did, little one. I am here always here. I am you, little one.* I gasped.

"Are you alright, Maria?" I looked at Ronan and

saw concern darken his green eyes. He met mine for a minute before nodding and lowering them.

"Why do you do that?"

"Do what?"

"You know what."

"I don't know what you mean. I do nothing, pri-Maria."

"I saw him."

"Him who?" He was only half listening to me. His eyes darted back and forth, taking in the chaos that surrounded us.

"Your Wolf."

"My Wolf? But how could you manage that? It's impossible."

I'd show him impossible. I reached out to my Wolf, that strange electric hum settling over me. I pushed it forward and called to Ronan with my mind. Shock and fear radiated from him. I could see his Wolf on the ground in my mind's eye and my Wolf stood tall over him. She yowled short and he stood to attention. *Yes, he will do.*

"Grazi? Hellooo!" I was brought back to where we were by a tug on my arm. It was Angela. "Earth to Grazi? You too, Ronan. What's going on?"

"We'll talk later." Ronan dropped his lunch into the nearest garbage can and hustled out of the gym without another glance. Considering the great appetite most Werewolves had, *me included*, this was like huge. I watched him leave with growing trepidation. *What the heck was happening to me?*

"What's his problem? Anyway, they think they've narrowed down who it is, did you hear?" Angela's anxiety translated to me in the way she gripped my arm and shuffled from one foot to another. Clearly, she was upset.

"No, I didn't hear anything new."

"Well, they think that it's Arnel Bayani. He was a senior. He was going to be valedictorian. It's so terrible! I knew him, Grazi, he wrote some stories for *NewsFlash*."

"Oh no, I mean I never spoke to him, but I know who you mean. That's awful, Angela." I could picture Arnel. He was tall with straight, dark hair and caramel colored skin. He wasn't a geek exactly. Sure, his grades were unbelievable, but he was also well liked socially. He wrote news articles, played soccer for the Zephyrs, though he was nowhere near the athlete Sebastian was. He was an all-around good person. He certainly didn't deserve to die like this.

"Yeah, well. I *knew* him, Grazi, we uh, we both play *Wolf Moon*. Sometimes we would meet up at Cyber-Sodas. He was pack."

"What uh, what are you talking about?" My hands started sweating and my heart began to pound. Did she just say *pack*?

"You never heard of *Wolf Moon*? It's an online role-playing game. You know, like Dungeons and Dragons. Except this is about Werewolves, vampires, witches and demons. You can build your own avatar and go to battle." Angela seemed to snap out of her melancholy when I said I didn't recognize the game. She spent the next ten minutes going over the finer points of *Wolf Moon*.

"Wow, it sounds intense, but I still never heard of it." I shrugged and tried to look nonchalant, but my mind was racing. I was sure there were loads of online role-playing games that involved the supernatural. Maybe it was just a coincidence that this game had something to do with Arnel's death. I bit into my protein bar and listened to Angela some more.

Those days I felt like such a heifer. I just kept eating and eating. Uncle Sean told me it was completely normal, my metabolism was super charged and therefore I would need to eat more. Still, he did recommend I try and eat healthy. Apparently, I have a very robust cousin named Gertrude who tipped the scales at well over two hundred pounds. So, yes, Werewolves, can get fat. That was one question answered.

"I mean I haven't played in weeks, okay well a couple of days, but I can't believe you never heard of it. What, do you, like, spend all of your time in your grandma's garden? Seriously! Anyway, for example, my avatar, Faolana-"

"Faolana?"

"Yes, *Faolana*. It means Wolf-girl. Yeah so, she's a Werewolf princess with special powers. She can change without the full moon to help her, she can mind chat with other Wolves, her sense of smell is like super acute, and she has the strength of seven Wolves. That just means I've been playing for seven years, the longer you play the stronger your avatar. Anyway, last time I played, I joined with another Werewolf who hunts witches. Together we saved this ancient village from disaster! It was real cool. And she's like totally hot. Faolana I mean, not the other Werewolf, anyway she's thin, but built with spiky red hair. Hey, I could show you!" I watched Angela's face turn pink in her excitement as she explained it to me, but I could hardly acknowledge her offer. I could practically feel the blood draining from my face. An online community of make-believe Werewolves that battled evil supernatural forces? Wow. That hit a little close to home.

"You know, it's weird though. As soon as I found out it was Arnel who died I checked online. His avatar signed in last night at nine and he was last seen heading into battle with BBWG, short for Big Bad Wolf Girl. She's like this new super avatar who's been kicking everybody's butt. She's been a loner up till now. Anyway, she asked him to join her at ten last night."

"So? They destroyed some make-believe things together? What does that mean?"

"That's just it. They didn't. He bragged about her invitation in his status updates then that was it. He didn't move again. And BBWG signed off shortly after. Anyway, meet me at CyberSodas later and I can show you. A bunch of pack hang out there. It's cool. You'll like it. We'll all want to say goodbye to *Gutum Lobo*, his avatar." I wasn't sure I'd like it, but still I agreed.

We walked to the auditorium together as the bell rang and Mr. Dennis' voice called the entire student body to assembly. Sebastian was waiting for me in the hallway.

"Hey Grazi, you heard?"

"Yeah, it's terrible."

"Yeah, hey Angela, sorry, I mean you knew him, right?" She nodded and we took seats near the back. Ronan was nowhere in sight. I scanned the room and didn't see his tall frame anywhere. Julianna and her clones were in a group, matching flat ironed hair and pink headbands on. They pretended to cry and held each other. *Jerks.* Fr. Verrell was there, he led us all in prayer and we stood up. When he was finished Sr. Diane approached the podium.

"Boys and girls, I am sure you all heard by now that there was a terrible tragedy last night. The remains of a body have been found on our campus. Now, please, do not go spreading rumors as they have not been positively identified-" I could smell her lying from across the room. I guess she thought she was doing what she had to for everyone's good. Her speech went on for a few more minutes. We were then allowed to call home.

School was dismissed a short while later, apparently too many parents were upset about the police activity and of course the dead boy. I made my way over to the Church basement, I figured I'd get to my lessons with Uncle Sean early. *Slow down, little one. Listen.* I slowed down in my tracks and closed my eyes. I listened and my mind seemed to travel with my hearing. If Angela spent years building up her avatar's super Werewolf powers, maybe I should try just using mine. I could make out two voices, Ronan and Uncle Sean.

"I'm telling you, sir, she heard my Wolf. Commanded him even."

"Tis impossible, Ronan. Too young. She hasn't even had her induction ceremony yet."

"Aye, but she's royalty and she's strong. Like *him*. What if it's her then? She could be doing the killing! We need to bring her to Rolf. He'll get her straight."

"No, don't you mention anything to Rolf! Do you hear me? We haven't had enough time yet. I must be certain. And don't you go putting ideas in her head! You're supposed to be watching her."

"I am trying, sir. What should I-"

"Wait, shhh! Grazi, are you there?"

I pulled back into myself and half walked half ran out of the Church. *He thought I was a murderer!* I was furious, scared, disgusted. How could Ronan even think that? How could my own uncle even consider the possibility that I killed people? I threw my book bag onto my back and started running. I didn't know where I was going. I jumped on the first bus I saw. Luckily, it took me to Main Street. I got off a few streets away from Cybersodas and started walking. I wasn't sure if I should still go or not. I mean, I could be a killer. *What if I was putting Angela in danger? Maybe I should head back.* Doubts swarmed my head. I was about to turn around when, *too late*, she saw me.

"Hey, Grazi! Come on!" She tugged me along with her and we entered the trendy little hybrid internet café meets old school ice cream soda pop joint. It was pretty cool actually. The whole place was done in bright reds and blues. There was a really long yellow bar complete with a huge stand-up freezer that showcased freshly made ice creams and frozen yogurts. Tall glasses, mugs, and bowls were behind the bar. There were old fashioned soda pumps cleaned to a brilliant shine along with rows of flavored syrups, bunches of fresh bananas, huge jars of maraschino cherries in three colors, sliced oranges, lemons and limes, and other toppings filling the huge counter space. Soda jerks dressed in crisp white aprons and little paper hats worked furiously to keep up with the crowd. Angela snagged us a booth and we waited for a waiter to come around. I would have appreciated the ambiance a bit more on any other day. *You know, any other day when I wasn't accused of being a murderer.*

"Hey there, ladies! The name's Derek, I'll be your soda jerk today. What can I get you?" I was still looking at the menu and had to bite my tongue when he said the word jerk. I almost didn't notice the increase in Angela's heart rate as she stared at the cute guy waiting to take our order. *Almost.* Derek had smooth mocha colored skin, his long dark hair was pulled back in a low ponytail and his wide hazel eyes sparkled as he and Angela discussed the day's specials.

"Well ladies, I want you to know that everything here is of the finest and freshest quality. We have some fresh organic frozen Greek Yogurt today in black cherry and plain tart. My specialty shake of the day is Kosta's Cherry Mix up, it's a hand shaken frozen Greek yogurt drink with black cherry cola, topped with fresh vanilla whipped cream and frozen sour cherries. What do you say?"

"That'll be fine. We'll have two of those and one hour of WIFI. How about some fries, Grazi?"

"Um, yeah, sure."

"And an order of sweet potato fries with cheddar cheese and chives, applesauce on the side. Thanks!"

"Just the way I like them! You got it, red!" He walked away, but not before winking at Angela which caused her to blush bright pink. *Sweet potato fries with cheese, chives and applesauce? So not what I was thinking when she said fries.* Anyway, I waited until she calmed down enough before asking about the game.

"So, who here plays *Wolf Pack*?"

"It's *Wolf Moon*, Grazi, and almost everyone. See that group there. They all wear green shirts because they're known as the *Verde Vanquishers*. Anyway look, just let me login here."

I watched as her fingers flew across her top of the line laptop's keyboard. For all that I knew about computers it was really a nice machine. I was still using a four-year-old Gateway Nonna picked up at a discount store. *Hey, it worked*. Anyway, Angela logged in and showed me the site, which turned out to be pretty cool. She even went so far as to create an avatar for me complete with my own login and password. Yup, I was *Wolfgirl2014,* very original. I doubted I'd use it again, but maybe I could learn something about Werewolves. It never failed to amaze me what a dork I am. I'm a Werewolf and I'd have to go to a silly game to learn about myself.

After we had finished our delicious milkshakes, *seriously awesome job Derek*, Angela's dad had a driver pick her up. Apparently, she was only allowed to take the school bus because it was early and considered safe, but her dad drew the line at other forms of public transportation and if he couldn't get her, a car service did. *Nice.* They dropped me off at home. I had too many things on my mind at the time to really think about what Angela had shown me. As far as I knew *Wolf Moon* was just a silly game and I, I was maybe a murderer. I entered the house quietly, I was hoping to make it up to my room unnoticed.

"Maria? Is that you?" I couldn't face my grandmother just then. I bit back a cry and took the stairs two at a time to my room. I should have known better.

A few minutes later there was a soft knock on my bedroom door.

"Maria, *bella*, can I come in?" The door opened and Nonna came in with a tall blue glass in her hand, she chuckled and held out the glass to me, "No Wolfsbane, *promiso*. It tastes very good."

I took the cup and sipped. Finally, some of my Nonna's awesome sweet iced tea. I broke down right then. The sobs shook my entire body, I slouched forward and put my head in Nonna's lap. She rubbed my back and murmured to me in Italian. I cried hard and long. For so many things. For my parents that I didn't remember. For Sebastian and the relationship I couldn't have with him. After all, how could I involve him in the horror that was now my reality? I cried for Angela, my new friend who would never speak to me again if she found out that maybe I killed Arnel. And selfishly, I cried for me. *It wasn't fair.* How was I supposed to control something I knew nothing about? As the sobs shook my body I thought of back when I was a kid. Always a good girl, I did my chores, went to Church, and studied hard. Why would God punish me like this? Was it true? Did I murder random people? Kill them in my Wolf form? Was I a monster? I had to know the truth.

"Nonna, please tell me what you know." I sat up and wiped my face.

"It is a long story, Maria, and a sad one, but I will tell you now." I straightened and looked at my grandmother as she patted down her springy gray curls and pulled her navy-blue sweater more securely around her. She took my hands and looked me in the eye.

"First Maria, I want you to know that I love you like I loved your mother before you, *capisce*? My daughter, Lilliana, was a beautiful young girl. Strong-headed like her father, but caring and generous. She had brown hair and warm eyes just like you." I shook my head. I've seen my mother's picture and she was very beautiful. She had had a certain grace and elegance that I seriously lacked. That much I knew. My grandmother didn't seem to notice my inner dialogue as she got caught up in the past. Her voice grew hard and bitter, or maybe I was picking up on her posture. *One more reminder of the freak I was now.*

"She fell in love with a boy. An Irish boy. Patrick Kelly. *Blonde* with a pretty face, pretty eyes. He convinced her he loved her. But he lied. He lied, Maria! His love for himself was bigger than his love for her. He kept a secret. A terrible secret. He could never be devoted to her because his loyalty was to his *pack*. She told me one night, the night you were born, Maria Graziana. She told me everything!" The anger and hatred that filled her voice frightened me. I could taste it. I growled and she looked at me startled.

"You wanted to know. Now, I tell you what I know. Lilliana told me the night you were born that you would be special. Ha, special! *Non especiale*, you would be cursed! The Bringer of Faith, the Defender of the Church, the Great Hunter. Pick a name, *cara*, they are all you. I didn't want this for you. He should have told her! Warned her! He should have left *mia bambina* alone. She didn't deserve this. You don't deserve this."

"You forgot to tell her something else, Rosa," I didn't jump. I had smelled Uncle Sean before he spoke.

"You forgot to tell her that Patrick didn't deserve this either! He didn't want any of this. Rosa, you know he wanted the best for Lilliana and for Grazi!"

"He knew it was possible, Sean. He knew he was cursing my daughter with endless worry and grief by marrying her! By giving her a child! By killing her!" I was dumbstruck. I had never heard my grandmother speak like this before. My heart sped up, I started to get hot, really hot despite the chill in the air.

"It was an accident, Rosa, dammit. Patrick loved Lilliana he never meant to hurt her. His change had never been like that! We never thought it possible! He lost himself to his Wolf before his reason came back."

"Lost himself, is it true? Did he kill my mom? Uncle Sean!"

"He never meant to hurt her. I swear it!"

"Is this what you meant when you said I was like him? Am I a murderer too? Is that what Ronan meant? Answer me!" My Uncle was now crouched on the floor lost in his tormented past. Nonna cried into her hands.

"It was the blood moon. Patrick-, your da, he never meant to- We were searching for a coven. There were signs. Your mum, she knew, she knew everything by then. You were three years old. She followed him, refused to stay home. The blood moon called and Patrick couldn't control-" Uncle Sean rubbed his face fiercely and I could feel his despair.

Nonna started swaying back and forth gripping her rosary beads and calling my mother's name one second and cursing my father the next. She and Uncle Sean argued some more, but by then I wasn't listening. *Who were these people anyway?* This man who was related to me, but absent my whole life and this stranger who raised me saying things I had never heard and could hardly believe. Pain shot to my gut and I knew what was happening, but for the first time I didn't fear it. I embraced it. I tore open the window and leapt onto the sill.

"Grazi!"

"Maria, no, wait!" Before they could stop me, I jumped to the ground, three stories below me. I landed on my feet and when I turned around I knew I was Wolf. I took off.

8

The moon was not yet full and I didn't understand anything about what had just happened. I only knew I was hurting. My Wolf came to take me away from my pain. She crooned to me in a language all our own. I felt safe and strong. It wasn't like we were two people, I wasn't schizo or anything. I was still me. One being with two aspects. I never felt so whole or complete as I did right then. I had felt my entire life like I was missing something. For a while I believed it was the result of being orphaned so young, but right then I knew. Yes, I missed them, but this bottomless void I couldn't fill had nothing to do with them. *It was her. It was me.* The other side of myself that I only recently discovered. I clung to my

Wolf and ran through the woods. I ran faster and faster. No destination in mind. I just had to get away.

Before I knew it, I was in the woods behind the school near the teacher's parking lot. I slowed down and panted, catching my breath. I thought I could run fast on two legs, but four carried me even faster. I scented something. It was rotten and foul. The smell was coming from a red Prius. That was a teacher's car. It was parked in the librarian's spot. *Jeez, Ms. Vorax must have hit a skunk or something.* It was awful. I sneezed and headed for the tracks. Everything was roped off by the police tape.

It didn't bother me, I simply jumped over the tape and walked until I stood in the spot where the body was found. All of the evidence had been collected by the investigators, but I couldn't shake the feeling I was supposed to be there. I sniffed around, my acute sense of smell even more powerful in my Wolf form. I could smell the grass seeds hibernating beneath the hard, frozen ground, insects, clay beneath the soil, ah, there it was. I could smell him, the poor dead boy, Arnel. I knew it was him because along with the sickly-sweet scent of death, there was also the unmistakable telltale odor of teenage boy. Chips, soda, and absurdly strong scented deodorant. I felt bad. Bad for his mother and father, his younger brother that I found out was in the local middle school, and I felt bad for Arnel. He died too young. Too violently. I could tell his death was bad by the amount of blood I smelled. It was strong and coppery. As I turned to walk away I caught a whiff of something. It was faint, but I could still smell it, a repugnant odor like skunk or a red fox I once smelled at Great Turtle Zoo. As quickly as I smelled it the scent was gone. I shook my long lupine head and headed for the trees. I heard someone coming. I looked towards the track and there he was.

Sebastian was bundled up in a fleece jacket, skull cap, gloves and sweats. He was running at full speed, puffs escaped his perfect mouth with each breath he took. I knew just how perfect that mouth was from the few times we kissed and before I could stop myself I ran over to him.

"Oh damn! Stay back!" Sebby sprang back from me and tripped. He landed on his butt on the cold hard ground. He held his hand out at arm's length and I realized he didn't know me. I was a Wolf for Pete's sake! *Way to go, Grazi!*

"Okay, you're okay. Just go back in the woods, giant scary doggy!" Sebby whispered, but didn't make any sudden movements. Wise of him, I didn't like being called a doggy and I growled at him to let him know it. I didn't want him to get hurt and to be truthful his fear was making me want to play with him a bit. I had to control myself. I howled and took off into the trees.

I still didn't want to go home. I was so angry. How could Nonna have kept these things from me? Did my dad actually kill my mom? So many unanswered questions playing over and over in my head. I didn't know if I was ready for the answers yet but it didn't stop me from wanting them.

Old habits die hard I guess because despite being a Wolf at the time I made my way over to the Church. Since I was a little girl any time I had a problem Nonna would take me to Church and tell me to pray for the answers. I would too, you know, do my praying or mental texting to God, or the Angels or Saints, or my parents. To whoever was best suited to answer my questions I guess. This time I knew exactly who I needed to talk to and it wasn't with prayer. The heavy wooden door that led inside the Church was propped open with an old brick. I could hear the cleaning crew working away scrubbing the old marble floors. A radio played classical music softly in the background. I made my way inside, careful not to make a noise. He was close. I could smell him. I headed down the corridor to the adjoining Rectory. That door was propped open also. I walked down the carpeted stairs to where the scent got stronger. This was it, his door.

I scratched at the old oak door with my large front paw. The sensation was strange, but I was getting used to it. The door opened and Ronan dropped the bottle of water he was holding. He wore a pair of pajama bottoms and a white tank top. Music blasted from a set of headphones still wrapped around his neck.

"Oh, shite! Maria, get in here!" Ronan pushed the door open wide for me then quickly shut and locked it. He was careful not to look me in the eyes. Good move on his part because I was not feeling too gracious. He took off his headphones and mp3 player and set them on his desk. I growled at him and he bent almost in half as if he were bowing to me.

"Okay, okay. Look, I'm sorry. Sean told me you heard. It's not what you're thinking though." I growled again, this time he fell to his knees and bowed his head. "Alright, look, Maria, I cannot talk if you force me to bend down like this. Please, I'm sorry. Let me up." Confused I stopped my growling. He sagged into a more comfortable sitting position almost immediately. His head was still cocked at a submissive angle and his eyes were on the floor. He was frustrated and nervous, I could tell by the set of his shoulders and by the scent coming off of him. Yeah, I can smell emotions. I'm such a weirdo.

"Can I look at you?"

"*What do you mean can you look at me? I'm right here you dope!*"

"No, I know you're right there, but I mean do I have your permission to look right at you?" He clenched his teeth as he asked. It must have really galled him. I simply didn't care. Too many things were happening and I didn't understand half of them. For a girl who was smarter than the average bear, or *Wolf*, I was frustrated beyond belief at this point. I needed to understand even just the tiniest of basics. Like *How to be a Werewolf for Dummies* or something.

"*Wait, can you hear me like this?*"

"Aye. I can? I mean, I can. Wow, I can hear you!" He straightened with the realization.

"*Okay, well, um great. Yeah, you can look at me.*" Ronan slowly turned his eyes, his head still cocked to the side. He held his hands up as if I were pointing a gun at him. He stared at me for a full minute then lowered his hands. He looked at me in my Wolf form with his intense green eyes. It was sort of like being naked before him. There was no way I could hide or lie about what or who I was, not like that.

"Beautiful." It came out a whisper from his lips,

but I heard it. He turned around quickly and grabbed a knit throw blanket from his bed.

"Here you'll want this now." He dropped the blanket at my feet, *er* paws just as I started to feel shaky. I didn't know what he meant, but then I felt a familiar crackle of electricity and a shiver started to crawl its way up my spine, gaining in intensity. I felt as if someone threw a punch to my backbone and I wondered for a minute if he didn't hit me. But then my skin stretched and my bones cracked. It wasn't exactly painful, but it wasn't as quick as my change to Wolf. *I'd have to work on that.*

It took me ten full minutes to change back. I was hot and my stomach was cramping badly. My bones stretched and joints popped until I was a girl again. My hair hung loosely around my shoulders and I shivered. Ronan turned his eyes down. He grabbed the blanket from the floor and wrapped it around my too sensitive skin gently as one would a newborn baby. "Oh," I groaned. It took me a minute to realize I was alone with a teenage boy in nothing, but his blanket. He was facing me too! I was paralyzed with embarrassment, and apparently deaf too. He was asking me something, but what? "What? Turn around, Ronan!"

"Okay, okay! Sorry. I asked you, if you needed anything?" He turned and faced the wall.

"Clothes would be nice." I mumbled as the shivering became uncontrollable.

"Yeah, um, bottom drawer behind you are some pants and shirts are second drawer. You know we, um run hotter than regular folks, but it's always a little colder going from Wolf to man, or, um, *girl*." He mumbled as I pulled out a pair of gray sweatpants and realized despite my height Ronan was much taller and much larger than me. I had to roll the waistband of his sweatpants three times to keep them from sliding down my narrow hips. Next, I found a long-sleeved thermal shirt and put that on. I found a pair of soft wool socks and stuck my ice-cold feet in them as well.

"So, was that your first time by choice then? How did it feel? Was it different than before?"

"I don't know. I don't remember anything about the first time I changed, I mean it's all hazy. My skin feels like I just rubbed it raw with a loofah or something." I fiddled with the sleeves on my borrowed shirt, soft as the cotton was it still irritated me.

"Oh well, yeah, I mean it is always a little tricky. You know, the change back. You were pretty fast though, ten minutes or so. Took me nearer to twenty minutes to change back for almost the entire first year. Now I'm down to eight or so. But, that was fantastic!"

"Fantastic? How do you mean?" I sat down on the

bed my teeth were chattering. I was freezing, Ronan held out the blanket I had dropped to me, an offering of sorts.

"Seeing you come in here like that. In your change, on a night when the moon is waning. It's fantastic! Incredible." His voice had dropped to a whisper and his other hand reached out as if to touch the blonde streak in my hair. He dropped it before touching me and I took the blanket and wrapped it around myself gently as I could. "You have a blonde streak down your muzzle, when you're Wolf. Did you get that your first time?" I nodded and self-consciously touched my hair. Julianna thought I was attempting to be like her and decided to streak my hair. *Whatever.*

"I got this my first time," he lifted his shirt and revealed a symbol on his chest just over his heart. It appeared to be a tattoo. A cross with a circle surrounding its center.

"We all get something. When I Wolf out I have dark fur in the shape of this on my chest. It's a variation of a high Celtic Christian cross. A protection symbol. Here I have it on this as well." He showed me a set of beads he wore around his neck. They were wooden and each carved with a different symbol. "My ma started this for me when I was born and every time I rise in the pack I'll add a new symbol. She made the beads out of wood from the *Tree of Saints*. It's sort of Sacred to us, Werewolves I mean. She went on a pilgrimage when she turned eighteen and took a stick that had fallen from the tree. Took her years to carve the beads. She saved them for her firstborn. *Me.*" He smiled at the memory. I reached out and touched his necklace.

"It's beautiful, Ronan. Do you have brothers and sisters?"

"Yeah, a sister, Margaret, she's a year younger than me, my brother, Daniel, is two years younger." I dropped my hand from his necklace.

"Why is it incredible to see me *changed* on a regular night?"

"The rest of us. We can only change during the full moon or on the Holy Days. I mean, we are always stronger and our senses more developed than regular folks, but you are the second Wolf I have ever heard of that can change at will and the first who seems to keep in charge as well." He seemed awestruck and his voice came out deeper than before.

"You mean my father, don't you?" Ronan looked away. "Tell me what you know, Ronan, please." I touched his arm. Instantly I could feel his sympathy. Hear his Wolf whine inside my mind. He was not the arrogant and aloof boy I knew from our shared classes or afternoon lessons with Uncle Sean. I closed my eyes and saw his large red Wolf. He howled in frustration, wanting to get to me, comfort me, protect me even. I was touched and something more. I think I may have been flattered. He broke the contact by stepping away.

"Please, it, it pains me not to be able to change with you now." He put a few feet of space between us. Not an easy feat considering the size of his room. It was painted plain beige and had a chest of drawers in one corner, a full-sized bed with an electric keyboard peeking out from underneath, and a desk that held a laptop and a small television set. A couple of free weights lined one half of the far wall. It seemed so bleak for a teenager's room.

"Maria, what I know are just stories. I don't know what is true and your Uncle Sean is not exactly forth-coming with me. Nor should he be. He is an impor-tant man in our pack. I'm not even a soldier yet. I'm still an initiate. I have yet to go through our formal rite of passage which I can only do when I turn eighteen. The only reason he brought me here was to see if the contract is valid."

"What rite of passage? Uncle Sean never mentioned it. And what contract?"

"As part of our rite of passage we have to go back to our village in Ireland where the pack elders will conduct a ceremony. It is like a Mass honoring God, during which we ask for His blessing and favor. After the Mass, there are several tests and the initiate has to pass. Each test designed to measure his or her own strengths and weaknesses."

"Are the tests physical?"

"Some of them. It depends on where you fit in the pack. Foot soldiers need to have their physical prowess tested, hunters their tracking skills, analysts need their wits measured, priests their faith and so on and so forth."

"Wow, I guess it is complicated." Bile rose in the back of my throat at the idea of being tested. But Ronan hadn't answered my other question.

"What about the contract you mentioned?" He rubbed the top of his head, making his strawberry blonde hair spike in every which way. It was kind of adorable.

"Listen, what's important now is you want answers about your father, yeah? Well I can tell you the stories I heard. You must understand they may or may not be exactly true. You see, your da, Patrick Kelly of the Pack Greyback, is something of a legend. I grew up listening to stories about him."

"Good or bad?"

"Depends. The men of our pack remember him

differently than the females. Must have been a heart-breaker, your da. Anyway, he was in line for pack Alpha. Good looking, strong and brave. It wasn't until he came to America and met your mum that things started to happen." I wanted to push for more information about this mysterious contract, but I was distracted by news of my dad. He was virtually a stranger to me. I desperately wanted to hear more.

"His change was becoming more attuned to his feelings and less to the phases of the moon. He could *change* at will! Now Maria, you have to understand, this was, no, this *is* virtually unheard of. Only legends remained of Wolves who could change at will and most of those were Wolves who had gone dark." He looked at me again and I could see he was a bit freaked out. *Yup, I'm a weirdo.* I felt numb as I waited for him to continue. "There are rules, laws for our kind." I shrugged and motioned for him to go on. *Rules, yeah I get it.* "Okay, I have been learning these things since well before my change. I've known what I am my entire life, you've had weeks to get acquainted with this side of yourself. It may take a while for you to understand." His discomfort was apparent. Like a billboard going off in the room, I had no choice but to ignore it.

"I'm not an idiot, Ronan, I can handle it. Please, I need to know." His eyes flared when I said his name and I could feel my own heartbeat increase in response. That time it was I who looked away from him. After a minute, he spoke again.

"Alright, I'll tell you what I know," His voice seemed a little deeper, his arrogance replaced by something else. "He was a great hunter, your da. Part of the job is investigating rumors or reports of covens and secret satanic societies. Your da had a better reputation than anyone for finding these covens and wiping them out. Normally the Hounds only go after a coven after getting the okay from the Church. But Patrick Kelly wasn't one to wait for approval. He was taking matters into his own hands. As he got stronger and his ability to change at will increased, he got reckless." Ronan was getting more and more agitated. His posture was stiff and his tone was clipped. I could *feel* his anxiety grow. I put my hand on his arm and he continued, a bit calmer. "He went after a rumor of the oldest of covens. The *Venetians*, a coven who worshipped the demon Moloch. Ridiculous really, I mean this was the stuff of legends. The Hounds had been seeking them for a thousand years. Rumor is they died out hundreds of years ago. The Hounds have not been active in hunting them for almost three hundred years now. But your father was certain it was them."

"Well, why would he believe it was them? He grew

up like you, he knew all the legends." I couldn't believe my father was the type of man who would chase a rumor with no proof, but then again, I didn't really know what type of man he was. Nonna always said I got my brains from my mother. She studied Church History and Mythology at NJ State University until before I was born. I remembered her books, still had some of them in boxes in the attic.

"There was a string of killings. Ritualistic murders. The Hounds to this day have not recognized it as the work of the Venetians, but your dad was convinced he had enough evidence to be certain it was them. He got others to believe him." I squeezed his arm encouraging him to continue. He looked into my eyes then and my heart skipped a beat. I saw anger mixed with grief so deep and profound that it hurt me.

"The four other Wolves he convinced to join him came here to the, U.S. They left their families for him," Ronan looked far away and so wounded it tore at my heart.

"If you want to stop don't worry, okay? Ronan, I'll understand." But he continued in a monotone. "They planned to sabotage the enemy's circle. Your ma for some reason followed him. It was odd, for a Hunter to not feel his mate's presence, but for whatever reason he didn't. When the Blood Moon rose they changed, all of them. They went in to get the coven, but it was a trap. Your dad was last to enter so he survived. The rest were destroyed in a fire cursed with witchcraft. Burned alive. Martin, his best mate, was first to go in. He was my father. I don't know why he left us on your father's word alone, but he did. I guess they didn't count on the enemy's strength." I felt responsible and horrified. My father had caused the death of his. No wonder he was so awful to me sometimes. I felt hot tears run down my face but made no sound or move to wipe them. Some tears just needed to fall.

"Whoever it was your dad found was onto him. They set him up. It has happened before, but not to a Hunter like him. Some said he was changed, not the same man they knew. Some said worse, others better. I don't know, I was young when it happened. My ma cried for so long. Her heart broke with her *matebond*. She was never the same."

"I'm so sorry, Ronan. For your parents and mine. I, I don't understand what happened. The *Blood Moon*? It doesn't make sense." My words came out a whisper. I turned away. I wanted to hide my tears, hide my weakness from him.

"The Blood Moon is the autumnal lunar eclipse. There is one every year. It's due at the end of next month. Different moons, phases, they are important to us." His voice sounded numb. His stance stiff.

"So, my mom followed him? How did she die?"

"Their bond should have alerted him to her presence. He should have *felt* she was there. We can only guess that in his agony at the death of his small pack, and the pain from his wounds that he got in the cursed fire, that he simply didn't recognize her. Half crazed he went at her. She was somehow thrown into the flames. There was no trace left of her. Your Uncle Sean has spent years trying to figure out what went wrong."

"Oh my God. I'm sorry, I'm so sorry, Ronan."

"I don't understand you, princess. You just find out your father murdered your mother and you tell *me* you're sorry? These are not your sins. You've no reason to be sorry. I should apologize to you, for bringing these horrors out into the open. It wasn't my place to tell y-"

"But I, I feel responsible!" Shame washed over me in waves. I felt impotent and enraged at my father's actions.

"Why should you? You didn't know anything about this." I couldn't believe how simply he said this. I was so inconsiderate and nosy to say the least, but he forgave me my father's sin as if it was the most obvious thing. I knew I could never repay him this kindness.

"What's a *matebond*?" I asked him, feeling humbled even in my shame. I felt stupid, ignorant even. It was an unfamiliar feeling for me and I didn't like it.

"Just like regular Wolves in the wild, we Werewolves choose one mate for the duration of our lives. However long God gives us. When we are mated whether it be to another Werewolf or a human, it doesn't matter, we form a *mate bond*. It is a connection, almost psychic if you want to call it that. Sometimes we can even speak to each other in our heads and feel each other's emotions. We can also give strength to one another through the bond. It is a most Holy union. The more honesty, faith, love and devotion for one another, the stronger the bond."

"It sounds beautiful."

"Yes, it usually is." Ronan continued to stare at me. *Beautiful, hmm.* I looked at the sharp angles of his face, his wide set eyes were by far his most attractive feature and they seemed to glow from time to time. His eyebrows, a few shades darker than his hair, arched naturally and I wondered why boys always seemed to be so perfect. Not one hair grew out of place, even the five o'clock shadow on his cheeks and chin seemed perfectly proportioned. His bottom lip jutted out slightly from his thinner top one and for a brief second, I wondered how they would feel. I knew I shouldn't be having thoughts about him, but I couldn't stop myself. I continued my observation.

He was muscular and tall. He had an elegance of carriage I wouldn't have attributed to someone his size. I guess it was the fact that he was a Werewolf that gave him such superb physical attributes and the grace to carry them off. But it wasn't his muscles that looked so good to me right then, it was his soul. I could see it in his emerald green eyes. His purity, his honor, his innate goodness. All these things were transparent to me. Not something I wanted to admit when I mostly considered him a pest who followed me around at school. For the first time since I knew what I was, I was getting answers. Real answers and he was the one giving them to me. So, I guess I could admit it even if only to myself, right then, Ronan was, in a word, extraordinary.

"So, that is the rumor, Maria. Your father never became a man again, at least that is what we were told. He transformed permanently to Wolf and was hunted down by our pack Alpha, Rolf. He's your grandfather actually." He broke eye contact and moved a few inches away from me.

For a few blissful moments, I looked into Ronan's eyes and everything else fell away, but now it was back.

I gasped as the impact of everything he had just revealed hit me. *My father murdered my mom! He was hunted down and killed by his own father?* My lineage was one of blood, violence, and sorrow. It was too much. I dropped to my knees and covered my face with my hands. Loud sobs shook my body as I poured out all my misery and confusion. I didn't feel it at first when Ronan sat directly behind me and placed his long legs around me. But then he wrapped me up in his strong arms. He held me tightly and murmured soothing words in my ear. In my mind, I could see our Wolves huddled together, his on the outside keeping mine safe. We stayed like that for a long while, until our hearts beat in time together.

Long after I had stopped crying he still held me. It felt so good. To be held and cared for. And to be told the truth for once. A knock on the door broke us apart. I could hear Ronan growl in annoyance and I smiled. *My protector.* Werewolf girls *so* didn't need protection, but it was nice even if a little old fashioned. I took a deep breath. It was Uncle Sean.

"Come in, Father Gallagher," said Ronan standing up and moving in front of me. My uncle walked in. He looked at our positions and smirked to himself.

"Ah well, you do know what your doing don't ya,

boyo?" His eyes flashed and for an instant I could see his Wolf.

"Aye, I do." Ronan averted his eyes, offering my uncle respect, but he made no move to back down.

"Good lad," he clapped Ronan on the shoulder and looked at me. "I'll never harm my niece, Ronan. That I can promise you. Are you alright, Grazi?" He rubbed the short beard that he managed to grow since I saw him a few hours ago and waited for me to speak.

"I'm fine, I guess. Why didn't you tell me about them?"

"I've been trying to find answers for a long time, Grazi. I know that what Ronan told you is what everyone believes I just can't help but think there is more to it."

"I guess that's why Nonna hates you and my dad. Because he killed mom."

"It's complicated, Grazi," His sorrow rolled off him in waves. Ronan and I both swayed a little in response. *Pack animals, got it.*

"Yeah, I'm sure it is. I'm going home." I stalked out of Ronan's room without a word of thanks. *I was such a jerk.* It must have been fine with him because he had his headphones on and his back to me. So much for our moment.

"Grazi, wait! I'll give you a ride. It's late." My uncle

followed me up the Church stairs. I waited for him to unlock the doors to Fr. Verrell's Mustang. I got in, put on my seat belt and waited for him to sit down and do the same. The car engine purred to life and Uncle Sean put the radio on low.

"There is something else I need to know, Uncle Sean. Will you tell me the truth?"

"Yes, of course, what is it?"

"All of those animal attacks, you know, the dead bodies? Was it me?" He shifted uneasily in his seat. *Hmm, he's nervous.*

"Grazi, as pack Beta I cannot make a formal announcement. As your uncle I can tell you, I don't believe you would knowingly harm anyone."

"You said *knowingly*."

"Don't worry, we will figure this all out, Grazi. Let's get you home." I nodded. I didn't need to tell him how I felt, I was sure he could read my emotions as easily as I read his. All that kept playing in my mind was that there was a chance, however small, that I didn't know what I was doing at the time? I really could be a murderer.

9

The night of the Harvest Dance I was seriously on edge. It was silly really. Given everything I had learned over the past few weeks, a *high school dance* had me biting my nails and dropping my books all day. I just wanted to be normal. I wanted to worry about normal things like my hair and what kind of music would they play. I ignored Ronan the rest of that week, or rather, *he* ignored me. He still sat by me during class, and continued to eat lunch with Angela and me, he just didn't talk to me. *Can you say silent treatment? Ugh.*

Sebastian and I managed to sit together at lunch that day despite Julianna's attempts at separating us. Since he was junior class president, Julianna had roped him into helping put up the decorations. Student

Council was important for his college applications, he explained to me, it made him look better, like he was into more than just sports. I understood completely. Even though I was a sophomore I realized my own applications would focus mainly on my academics. *Maybe I should take Coach Vinnie up on his offer and try out for the girls' soccer team?*

Sebastian spent most of the day with Julianna and the rest of the cheering and soccer teams. They had been excused from their classes in order to set up for the dance. It was okay though, I wasn't jealous. Well, I wasn't *too* jealous. I mean given the differences between Julianna and myself it was a wonder Sebby actually wanted me as his date. I mean sure, we jogged together and yes, he was the first boy to have ever kissed me. I just kept wondering why. Why *me*? Technically, I was a sophomore, and a geek on top of that. I was not beautiful or dainty like the other girls. Just about everyone in school had a crush on Sebastian. He had his pick. All of the freshmen broke out into hysterical giggles when he walked by. A few of the girls in my homeroom class even congratulated me on him asking me to the dance. *Can you believe that?* I picked at my chef's salad as Sebastian ate his sandwich with gusto.

"So, are you all set?"

"What do you mean?"

"I don't know I guess all the girls keep talking about dresses and going to the salon and stuff so I thought I'd be polite and ask. Oh, what color are you wearing? You know for the wrist corsage?" I looked at him blankly. I never even considered this stuff. To be honest I thought I would wear my graduation dress from eighth grade. It was off white with little crystals sewn into the bodice. And my hair? Oh Jeez! It would be a disaster!

"Um, it's shiny, like off white?" It came out more of a question than an answer, but he just smiled and kept eating. *Crap!* I guess I had to get him a flower too. I'd have to see if we had any roses left after being hit by that drought and then the frost. Sebastian finished his sandwich just as Julianna came to get him.

"Come on Sebby, we have to go. Now, please." She gave me a dirty look as Sebastian bent to take his tray. He gave me a brief kiss on the cheek and tugged on my ponytail playfully.

"I'll see you tonight, Grazi," he said before turning to walk away.

It was a *very* public kiss, regardless of how small. Some of the girls fanned themselves when I caught their eye and a few others sent me high fives from across the room. *Yeah, I was definitely beet red at this point.* Sebby had pretty much just publicly declared that we were, well, *something*. I felt eyes on me, but when I turned to glance at Ronan he was chewing what appeared to be half of one of his three double cheeseburgers in one bite and acting as if nothing was wrong at all. In fact, he had been acting as if our interlude the other day had not happened. Maybe it hadn't. Maybe I was exaggerating it. I wished I had someone to talk to. So, I did what I would normally do, I talked to my parents.

Hey, it's me. So, I guess you know that I know I'm a Werewolf now. I would have liked a little heads up, guys seriously. I guess what I want to know is are you guys there? Daddy are you in Heaven with mom? Even after...Never mind. Well, whichever one is listening, I think I am having a crisis. A normal teenager crisis I guess, not a Werewolf one, and it is probably not important, but what do you do when you think you like two different boys? Is it possible? Maybe that means I don't like either of them? Any advice would be great. Oh, and what do I wear to a school dance? I sound like such an idiot, I'm sorry. I'm sure you have more important things to do. Never mind. I love you. Xxoo

"Hey Grazi, what time are you getting to the dance?" My thoughts were interrupted by Angela. She seemed to be in a good mood and was busy talking about her date and her spa appointment for after school.

"I'm going to get a mani-pedi and of course a facial before the dance. I'm going to *Earthly Glow Spa* over on Route 46. They are clients of my dad's law firm. Where do you usually go?"

"Um nowhere, I mean, I've never been-" Ronan snorted and I gave him a dirty look. I could feel my Wolf growl and he looked sick for a moment. Then he got up and tossed his tray. I was happy he was leaving. *Jerk!*

"What? No way, that's it! You are *so* coming with me! My dad's sending a driver and I know Sherry will take you no problem!"

"No, Angela, it's okay, besides I'm tapped out right now."

"No worries. It's on me! I insist Grazi, besides I *hate* to go alone." I kept turning her down and was surprised when at 4:00 I was up to my eyeballs in a mud mask, my hair had been neatly trimmed, and I was getting a manicure. I insisted they did not cut my nails and was a little embarrassed when I broke three nail files. *Werewolf nails are super strong.*

"This package must be faulty, let me get another," the manicurist was a slight woman no older than twenty-two and I felt sincerely sorry for all the broken nail files. Since my change, my nails had grown a lot longer than I was used to and they were much stronger than usual too. No way could they be cut with regular clippers and it seemed filing was difficult too. I decided to tell her it was no use when she came back with a pumice stone instead. It worked fine and in no time, I had a French manicure and pedicure to match.

Angela and I were getting the mud rinsed when the owner of the spa came in and did a review of my face, noting in particular my eyebrows. "You know, Angela, your friend here could use a little zap, how about it, yes?" She spoke with a slight accent and Angela giggled in response to her question.

"Okay now Grazi, forgive Sherry here, I told her over the phone I would be bringing you in and that I thought you should have a few *treatments*-"

"Angela, I can't afford it. And besides I never even waxed before. What does *zapped* mean? Doesn't it hurt?"

"I told you it's *on me* and we weren't thinking wax." She looked up at the ceiling, at the floor, anywhere but at me and I had to wonder why. I never really cared about my appearance before so no, waxing was not something I did, and since becoming a Werewolf, I admit I probably should have.

Without any explanation Sherry wheeled in a

wicked looking machine and some crazy sunglasses. After twenty minutes of being zipped and zapped by the laser hair removal machine thingy, I had not one hair out of place anywhere on my face. My eyebrows looked great and apparently my mustache, which I didn't even realize I had, was gone as well. Apparently being a Werewolf meant more facial hair for guys and girls especially as we neared the full moon. That explained the scruff on Ronan's face and Uncle Sean's full-grown beard. The full moon was coming tomorrow night. Uncle Sean explained that with the dance so near the full moon he, Ronan, and myself would all be drinking tea laced with Wolfsbane before nightfall. I had carried mine with me all day in school and forced myself to drink the bitter liquid. I stared in the huge gilded mirror at my smooth face.

"Put this cream on and the redness will go away, yes. You did good. No crying like some other people." Sherry gave Angela a look and she just smiled back. She handed me a tube of cream and a small sample bag of cosmetics along with a brochure of their services. I turned and hugged the shorter woman.

"Thank you," I whispered.

"Oh nonsense," she was flustered, but pleased. I could tell, "Now you come back anytime! You don't have to wait for Angie, okay dear!" I nodded and left with Angela. Her driver dropped me off at a quarter to five. I thanked my friend and told her I'd see her later. Fifteen years old and my first trip to a spa/salon. I felt pretty happy and yes, a little nervous too. This was a year for a lot of firsts.

I was excited, but also saddened by the fact that Nonna still wasn't talking to me. She had given me a wide berth since the night I learned about my parents. She even started leaving my dinner on a plate on the stove, not bothering to wait and eat with me as was our usual custom. She no longer asked me to Mass with her or to watch *Jeopardy!* In fact, we hadn't talked in what felt like forever. I really missed her. She was the one who raised me and loved me. She was the only real home I knew. I felt guilty, but I was still so very angry at her. Angry at her for concealing my past. Who and what I was. That afternoon when I got home from the spa there was a gift box on my bed. It was pretty big and printed with roses, topped with a big pink bow. Taped to the outside I found a letter:

Mia cara Maria,

I have loved you and protected you for so long I don't know how to stop. Perhaps you can forgive an old lady's clumsy attempt to keep what is left of her only daughter safe. I made you this dress from a pattern I saw on that soap opera we used to watch together. But that is not the most important thing I give you. Here is a diary your mama kept. I have not read it. I cannot bring myself to, but maybe there are some answers for you, si? Ti amo, mia bella bambina. Always, Nonna

Tears sprung to my eyes as I put the letter down. I opened the box and lifted a dress out of the careful packaging. To say it was beautiful would be a gross understatement. It was more than beautiful. Certainly, the fanciest piece of clothing I had ever owned. Impossibly soft gold lace sewn over a nude lining. It shimmered and seemed to glow every time I handled the exquisite fabric. The bodice was fitted with short cap sleeves and a boat neckline. The slip didn't start until it covered my chest leaving my shoulders and back covered only in the delicate gold lace. A soft and flirty skirt that stopped just above my knees completed the lovely confection.

I held it against me and inhaled. I could smell my Nonna on it. Under the dress was a pair of shiny nude wedge heels with the same gold lace sewn just over the toes. I knew she must have spent hours laboring over this for me. I could almost feel the love she poured into it with her strong hands. It was the first occasion I had to get dressed up like this and I was thrilled with it. *Truly.* I was so excited about the dress and shoes. I almost overlooked the treasure beneath them.

My mother's diary. As thick as any Bible, the cover was a soft white leather with the name Lilliana Maria DiPaolo etched in gold. I opened the diary and found myself staring at a collage of pictures that had been carefully cut and glued onto the cover page. A newborn baby held by an older boy, obviously my mom and uncle, her in her school uniform, Nonna and Nonno, snapshots of her friends, my mother and father at what had to be prom and more of the same. It was *amazing*. I turned to the first page and saw a table of contents. She marked each year that she wrote in the diary and what page that year started on.

To my surprise I found she had kept this same diary up until the year she died. She started it when she was fifteen years old. The same age as me. The same year she met my dad. I took a deep breath and put the book in the drawer of my nightstand, under my rubber duck inspired lamp. I wanted nothing more than to stay in my bedroom, on my rubber duck blanket and read the entire thing cover to cover. But tonight was special. *One thing at a time, Grazi.* Plenty of time to read later. When my head wasn't dancing in so many directions. Speaking of dancing. I headed towards the bathroom. It was time to get ready.

Though I suggested we meet at the school gymnasium where the dance was being held, Sebastian insisted on picking me up. Julianna had stormed over to Lizette's house. She swore she would never stand by to watch me get picked up by her man. *Okay then, delusional much?* Aunt Theresa glared daggers at me for days and wouldn't even acknowledge me otherwise. Thank goodness, she was already waiting in the car to bring Julianna over to Lizette's by the time I got home. I have to say on my list of things I cared about, her feelings about me ranked pretty low.

At seven o'clock sharp the doorbell rung and Nonna answered. I played with my hair, deciding to leave it down was risky. It was so long there was a chance I'd get lost in it, but I shrugged. Too late to change now and with my new trim it was shiny and soft. I was not used to heavy make-up and now that I was a Werewolf I think I was even more *aware* of it than ever. I mean I could literally smell the chemicals my cousin put all over her face from a room away. That night I wore just a hint of glitter on my eyelids, a touch of brown mascara that was in the samples bag from Sherry. I completed my look with a cherry flavored ruby lip gloss that I applied lightly over my lips. When I looked in the mirror I couldn't get over the changes in me. I looked okay. *Really* okay.

"Maria, your date is here." Nonna knocked shyly and opened my door. "Oh *si, si si, bella! Molto bella*!"

She clapped her hands together and wiped a tear from her eyes.

"Oh Nonna! Thank you so much. You know for everything." I had to stop myself from crying.

"We will talk later, Maria, now you go. Your young man is waiting." I hugged her small frame and kissed her cheek before walking downstairs.

"Wow," Sebastian waited for me by the door and almost dropped the wristlet he held in a clear plastic box in his right hand. He wore a dark suit with a patterned tie. It had flecks of gold in it, so we *kinda* matched.

"You look beautiful," he whispered as I got closer to him.

"Thanks, um, you do too."

"This is for you. You said off white, but I think it still matches." He took the wristlet out of the box. A mixture of yellow baby's breath, yellow speckled orchids and red roses with lush green accent leaves, it was perfect. He placed it on my wrist and smiled.

"Thank you, it's beautiful. This one is for you." I picked up the one white rose I salvaged from the bushes outside. I had carefully wrapped the single stem and few accent leaves in some of my uncle's floral tape. I managed to pin it to his jacket without impaling him, so that was good.

"My dad's outside so we should get going," A flash snapped and we both jumped then laughed. Guess we were both nervous. Nonna took another four pictures on her ancient camera before she let us escape.

The drive to the school gym in Sebastian's dad's black Mercedes was short and a little awkward. His dad kept looking at me in the rearview mirror and rubbing the gold and diamond crucifix around his neck. He was young for the dads in our school, probably the same age mine would have been, mid-thirties or so. Most of the other dads were late in their mid to late fifties. Mr. De La Cruz, kept looking at me and it was giving me the creeps. Sebastian must have noticed.

"Dad!"

"What? Oh! So, uh, Maria, what was it your dad does again?"

"Oh, my dad passed away Mr. De La Cruz when I was very young. I live with my grandmother and my uncle's family."

"Dad!" Sebby scolded him from his seat next to me in the back.

"Oh, um, I'm sorry for your loss then." I nodded and sat in silence. Sebastian held my hand and tried not to be embarrassed by his dad's behavior. Mr. De La Cruz was sending some seriously whacky vibes. I could smell his nervousness, though why he'd be nervous with me I didn't know.

"Okay, here we are kids. Sebby, I'll be back at eleven. You two behave. Call me if you need anything, son."

"Sure, Dad." Sebby held the door open for me and I got out of the car. I was glad I wore a jacket over my dress. It had dropped to about thirty degrees since that afternoon. I smiled at Sebby and waved goodbye to his dad.

The first thing I saw when I entered the gym was this huge Cornucopia made out of tissue paper and glitter with huge paper and glitter fruits and veggies coming out of it plastered on the left wall. On the right-side wall was a large banner that read "SHPS Annual Harvest Dance." This had Julianna and her clones stamped all over it. There were huge clumps of balloons in red and orange and yellow all throughout the gym as well as a strobe light and fog machine.

Despite the cheesy decorations, the DJ was actually good. Anthony Monroe and his older brother Rob worked a laptop from between two turntables and some sort of mixer stand. It looked complicated, but they seemed to know what they were doing. Anthony was in my homeroom and Rob graduated the year before. Sebastian checked our coats and walked us over to the picture booth where we got in line for a picture to commemorate the evening. I was laughing at something he said when I tensed up.

I turned around. *Of course.* Ronan was behind me. He had on black pants and a black shirt with a jacket over it. *Fancy.* Then I looked down. He was wearing beat up green Converse instead of dress shoes. His hair was casually spiked, a thin fuzz covered his chin and cheeks, and he had his string of beads around his neck. He looked good. He didn't meet my gaze, but instead seemed to look past me.

"Hi, Ronan."

"Maria." He nodded but still didn't look at me. His posture was stiff, I could almost hear him humming with energy. One night till the full moon, his Wolf was tense and ready to go. *This was so not good.*

"So, who are you here with?" I tried to break the ice. Sebastian took my hand and squeezed it. He nodded a greeting to Ronan. *Boys.*

"Why? Don't you think I have a date?"

"No, I didn't say that-" I stopped abruptly when he turned back to grab his date. Julianna was right there her clone army standing behind them along with Sebby's teammates, Tyler and Mike. We nodded our hellos and Julianna wrapped her hand possessively around Ronan's arm and flashed me a dirty look.

"Hellooo! The line is moving! People wanna dance not just stand here all day." She rolled her eyes and her groupies snickered. I tried not to stare but couldn't help it. Sure, she invaded our lunch table more often than not, but I thought it was all for Sebby. I had no idea she was into Ronan as well. It really bothered me. *Ugh*. I hated to admit it, but she looked great too. She wore a black sparkly dress, strapless and skintight. Her heels were about five inches high and as always, she wore her hair and make-up perfectly. As if she stepped off a cover of a magazine. *Fabulous*.

"Our turn," Sebby said casting curious looks at Ronan. Ronan grinned at Sebby, but not in a friendly manner. I could practically hear his thoughts. He wanted a fight. He didn't seem to notice his date's company, not even when she leaned up against him with her whole body. She got bored when he failed to react and turned to talk to her friends. I stepped on Ronan's foot to get his attention, he didn't even budge. A low growl escaped his lips.

"What are you doing?" I whispered in a voice so low only with his Werewolf hearing could I be heard.

"That hurt."

"Good. Now stop growling at my date and pay

attention to yours. She's just dying for you to compliment her." I'll admit it I was hurt. He knew I couldn't stand my cousin, didn't he? Why would he go with her of all people?

"Is she now," Ronan turned and placed his nose against Julianna's neck. Was he *sniffing* her? *She is so gonna slap him!* Instead I was surprised when she giggled and he gave her a slight peck on the cheek, "You smell awful good, girl."

"You like? I put it on *everywhere*!" She said seductively and batted her long eyelashes. Her arm wound even tighter around his bicep. He grinned and bit his lower lip. *Oh yuck.* I turned around ready for my picture with my date. I didn't stay to watch Julianna plaster herself all over Ronan. It made me nauseous.

"Come on, let's dance." Sebastian led me to the dance floor. With my heels, I was a little bit taller than him and I felt really awkward. *Why was I so darn tall?* He didn't seem to care, he spun me around until I lost all of my silly self-consciousness. We jumped up and down and danced to all of the fast songs. When a slow song came on he took me in his arms and pulled me close to him.

"This is nice. I like dancing with you, Grazi." I stared into his warm brown eyes and felt something inside me melt. His full lips curved in a smile and I could hear his heart beating in his chest. He kissed my hand and wrapped it around his own.

"This feels right, you know? You and me." He placed it on his chest between us. It was the most perfect moment of my life, until…

"Leave room for the Holy Ghost," Sr. Diane said and abruptly pushed us apart. My cheeks burned and Sebastian put his hands in his pockets. Seriously, that was one scary nun. Where did she come from anyway?

"Um, maybe we should go get something to drink?" He asked and I noticed the pink stain on his cheeks.

"Good idea," I said and followed him to the refreshment table. Ms. Vorax and Mr. Gundy, the history teacher, were getting refreshments also. Ms. Vorax looked so small and childlike in her straight gray dress and slip-ons. Especially next to Mr. Gundy and his robust figure.

"Hi Ms. Vorax," I said with a smile. She turned her large gray eyes on me briefly and smiled vacantly. She was too busy staring at Mr. Gundy and, *ew*, wait a minute, she looked like she was captivated by him. I mean the guy wore too small plaid pants, suspenders and a bow tie every day to class and this dance was no different. He patted his belly and moaned in delight as he bit into a brownie and offered one to Ms. Vorax.

She shook her head and handed him another one. She didn't seem to notice the huge coffee stain on his shirt or the fudge stuck in his teeth. *Yuck.* But there was no accounting for taste. Look at Ronan and my cousin. He was twirling her on the dance floor and she was swaying seductively and rubbing all over him. *Yuck, where was Sr. Diane when you needed her?*

"So, what do you think of the dance?"

"Oh, it's great. Thanks for asking me to come with you, Sebastian. I'm having a really good time."

"No problem. I missed you this week. You know, running with you. But I guess you're the sane one. It's so cold now I can't even imagine what it will be like in a few weeks." I smiled and only half listened as Sebby continued to take sips of his water and talk about the weather and his soccer training. I made all the proper noises, but the truth was I was distracted.

"Do you smell something?" I took a deep breath and there it was again. That repugnant odor. I looked around, Sebby didn't seemed to notice it, he shook his head no. We were alone. No one was near the refreshment table now. Ms. Vorax and Mr. Gundy had wandered off and looked like they were going back into the school. It was off limits to the students during the dance.

"Nah, I don't smell anything. Hey, I guess Ms.

Vorax and Mr. Gundy are sneaking away together." Sebby laughed and nodded at the door. "What do you think she sees in the guy?"

"Who? Mr. Gundy? Seriously, I have no idea."

"Yeah, pretty gross thinking about teachers making out anyway." We laughed some more. Sebastian took my hand and gave it a little squeeze. He made me feel special and normal all at the same time. Not like a freak or anything. To him I was just a girl. I wanted to forget the weird smell, the deaths, *everything*, except being with him. I couldn't wait to see what the night would bring.

"Hey Grazi!" I turned to see Angela run up to me and throw her arms around me in an exuberant hug. "Wow you look fabulous! Where did you get that dress?" Angela said hi to Sebby and raised her eyebrows up and down. She was such a loveable nut job! She was wearing bright green which sort of clashed with her bright orange hair but seemed to work just the same. "Don't you love this color? I saw it in a boutique by Daddy's offices and I just fell in love with it! I was so happy it fit! Oh, this is my date Darrin. Darrin say hello."

I looked over at the chubby blonde guy standing behind her. He wore a beige suit and thick glasses and seemed very nervous. Angela leaned into me and whispered "He goes to St. Pious, and he wants to intern at my dad's offices over the summer. Daddy made me take him to the dance to size him up. I figured why not? LOL! Oh no, here comes your cousin and the clones. Do they go anywhere without her?"

"Hey Sebby, my date had to excuse himself for a minute. Do you think you could help me with the sign? It needs more tape." She completely ignored my presence and literally grabbed his hand out of mine. I'm not proud of it, but I wanted to knock her on her butt.

"Um hello, he's here with Grazi, you know." Angela was gaining a little confidence since the beginning of the year and I was grateful for her coming to my rescue like that. It was really sweet.

"Oh, did you come here with her? I thought you were alone. Anyway, it's for the school decoration committee. Like, where is your school spirit anyway, Anna?"

"It's Angela."

"Yeah, uh huh. So, Sebby, can you help?" He looked from me to Julianna, clearly unsure what he should do. I decided to be a good sport and let him off the hook.

"Go ahead. I'm fine."

"You sure?" I smiled though it didn't reach my

eyes. I mean I *was* annoyed. He asked me one more time if I was sure and I nodded. He kissed me briefly on the lips and walked away. Julianna latched onto his arm like a parasite. I let out a frustrated sigh.

He was at the dance with me. He could have asked her, but no he asked me. Ronan asked her. Ronan. Hmm. Where was Mr. Tall. Irish and Brooding anyway? I scanned the room and didn't see him anywhere. Another quick scan and bang, there he was walking through the same doors Mr. Gundy and Ms. Vorax went through previously. I excused myself from Angela and her date and followed him.

"Hey Ronan! Wait for me. What's up?"

"Oh, can you leave your *Prince Charming* for a second and do your job now, princess?" *Great, we were back to that now.*

"Give me a break, Ronan. What about you and Julianna?"

"She's well fit, that girl."

"Yeah, well, whatever. What's our job anyway? The full moon isn't until tomorrow night."

"Yeah, well, sometimes we can't wait for it. Besides I'm only investigating." I had to speed up to keep pace with Ronan's long legs. Yes, I was faster and taller than most people, but he still had a good five or six inches on me. At least I didn't feel awkward about my height with him. Heels and all he still towered over me.

"Investigating what?" I looked at him and saw his eyes flash as he took a deep breath.

"You smell that?"

"Yeah, I thought it was just dead mice in the walls or something."

"It's something alright. Death, but not mice. Not anything I've ever smelled. And it's moving."

"Are you sure? I've smelled that before, but I didn't know what it was."

"Where? When?" he stopped and grabbed my arm, looking at me for answers.

"The night I came to your room, when I was *you know*. I stopped by where they found the body and sniffed around. That smell was all over the ground and by the teachers' parking lot."

"Why didn't you tell anyone?"

"Like who? I thought it was an animal or something!"

"Alright, alright, let's go." He tugged me along with him. We tracked the smell to the library where it was strongest. There were faint noises coming from inside. I hesitated, but Ronan, he opened the door. He had courage. I'd give him that. He put a hand in front of me and stepped inside the dark room. We didn't need to turn on the lights. Wolves are nocturnal. If anything, I could see better in the dark. He put up a hand for me to hang back as we slowly made our way inside. I grabbed at Ronan's arm. I could hear crunching, like the sound an animal makes when feeding. Whatever it was, it was crunching on something loudly and it smelled like the wrong end of a skunk.

Ronan crouched down alongside a bookshelf. We were in the biographies section actually. I didn't need my Werewolf senses to know that. I had re-shelved books in that section almost all of the previous week. Mrs. Theodore always assigned a biography report to the freshman every September, it had been due that Monday. The chomping sounds were louder on the opposite side of the room. I leaned over Ronan and almost lost my balance. He put his hand on my stomach, righting me. But not before I got a good look. There was a *thing* on the other side of the library and it was chewing on something. *Oh Jeez!* It was a foot.

We couldn't see anything else from that vantage point. I had an idea. I poked Ronan. He looked at me, one perfect eyebrow arched in question. "Lift me up," I mouthed and pointed to the top of the shelf. Ronan understood immediately. His eyes glowed briefly as he grasped my waist and lifted me straight up as if I weighed nothing at all. I got a good look from up there.

This *thing* was tearing at some poor animal. It had a leg in its mouth and was shaking it ferociously. I could finally make out the shape of what it was attacking. It was a person! A man! I could just make out Mr. Gundy's prone form, his hideous plaid pants ripped to shreds as the beast shook his leg in its mouth. He was unconscious but I think I heard him breathing.

The creature was the scariest looking thing I had ever seen. It had to be over seven feet tall. I could tell even crouched on all fours as it was. It was definitely humanoid in shape, excruciatingly thin with its rib bones clearly defined and shoulder blades protruding from under its pale grayish skin. It had huge antlers on its head like a deer or elk. It was making crunching and slurping noises and that's when I realized it was *eating* Mr. Gundy alive! My Wolf came to attention in my mind and snarled. *Danger!* Ronan put me down without making a sound. His expression was a mixture of awe and horror. *Right.* My Wolf spoke directly to his of what she saw and now he knew. We had to figure out what to do. Ronan couldn't turn Wolf yet. He wouldn't until tomorrow night's full moon. I saw his determination and before I could stop him he gently pushed me down to sitting position, then he let out a yell and ran full speed at the creature. He knocked into it with his shoulder and it dropped Mr. Gundy's leg with a careless thud.

The creature jumped back and crouched to attack. Its face was horrible. Emaciated, sunken in cheeks with huge, hollow, gray eyes. *Familiar* gray eyes. Its razor-sharp teeth dripped blood as it screeched. It raised its claw-like hands and raked them across Ronan's chest making a wet, slicing sound like Nonna did when she cut and wrapped meat for the big freezer in the basement. It made me gag. Ronan howled in pain and I saw his ruined shirt darken with blood. His blood. He managed to shove the creature off. It slammed against the librarian's desk with a *crack*.

Ronan struggled to stand. I could tell he was in pain before I heard his strained gasp. His eyes locked on mine as the creature rose to its full height. The thing shoved the desk in anger and it slammed against the far wall causing the lights to flicker. The shadow it cast was gargantuan and I trembled. *I could die here. Tonight.*

"Run Maria! Get out of here!" Ronan looked around for a weapon. He picked up a chair from one of the tables that were set up around the library and flung it at the creature. The thing carelessly swatted the chair out of the way and made a noise out of its cruelly twisted lips, something like laughter.

I was ashamed as I stood there. Helpless. Ever the protector, Ronan's only thoughts were to get me out of there. *Help him. I can help him. Let me help.* It was my Wolf. I could see her in my mind's eye. I had been paralyzed with fear, but the minute she spoke I found courage. I nodded to myself, I knew what I had to do. I yanked my dress over my head and stuffed it in the nearest bookshelf. I kicked off my shoes and crouched down. Clad only in my bra and panties I closed my eyes. I forced air in and out of my nose as I concentrated. The rancid stench of the thing filled my nostrils as did the scent of fresh blood. *Come on, come on, come on.*

Another piercing howl from Ronan's lips. I looked over at him and lost my focus. The thing had him in its claws. He was struggling to get it off. Its jaw unhinged, revealing row after row of jagged teeth that gleamed like razors in the fluorescent light coming from the lamppost outside the windows. It attempted to bite down, but luckily Ronan ducked out of its grip. He almost escaped unscathed, were it not for one particularly long fang that scraped him across his cheek. He staggered. I didn't know how much longer he could last. Blood loss and getting knocked around was tiring him quickly.

Oh, God no! I squeezed my eyes shut. *Concentrate, damn it!* I cleared my mind and let instinct take over. Finally, I felt it. Like I had just grabbed hold of a live wire. Electricity and heat flashed through me. I opened my eyes and could feel power radiating through my body. One minute I was on two legs, the next I was on four. A massive Wolf with a platinum streak down my muzzle. Larger than any Wolf in the wild, I growled and lunged just as the creature screeched and opened its mouth. Ronan fell to his knees under its weight. The creature was too wrapped up in its attack to hear me. I knocked it off of Ronan with my huge paws and crouched down for another attack. I growled at Ronan to move away and he did, staggering away as fast as he could. Shock and awe apparent on his face.

I had practiced fighting on two legs, but not four. I was sure my Werewolf reflexes would take over. At least I *hoped* they would. Large, empty, gray eyes looked me over. I kept thinking they were familiar. *Too slow Grazi, wake up!* I barely missed getting my eyes scratched out by the thing as it lunged for me. A quick tuck and roll and I came up ripping and slicing with my own razor-sharp claws across its hideous back. The creature shrieked as its gray skin peeled open to reveal noxious black blood and yellowish bone, no meat at all. I saw Ronan crawl over to Mr. Gundy in my peripheral vision. He was shaking the teacher then going through his pockets. I think he pulled out a cell phone. I had no time to think about what he was doing. The creature hissed and came at me again.

I ducked and ran again, circling the creature. The hunger in its hollow eyes frightened me. I couldn't seem to get past its defenses. It always seemed ready for me to strike. It used its antlers to butt me out of the way. As the seconds passed my muscles settled into a rhythm of running, ducking, clawing and lunging. I managed to avoid getting bitten, but its claws raked me once across my foreleg. It stung and I smelled my blood. I was getting tired of the ducking and running.

It was time for me to face the thing. *Use its hunger, little one. Trap it with its weakness and we will vanquish this demon.* My Wolf spoke to me and I could feel her energy flow through me. Suddenly I *knew* what to do. It's not as strange as it sounds. Like having your conscience take a voice I guess. The thing's patience had clearly run out. Its tongue snaked out and it seemed to be licking its lips before lunging wildly. I stopped running. I pretended to favor my paw where it had scratched me.

It gnashed its teeth and charged. But this time I

was ready. I pushed off of my hind legs and locked my own four-inch-long fangs around its thin neck. As I squeezed I heard a crack and realized I had crushed something. I spit out the foul thing and stepped back, still in Wolf form. The creature wheezed and made choking sounds. It changed right in front of me. It went from monstrously tall and emaciated, to petite and dainty in a space of a few seconds.

"Finish me! Please," I could barely make out the words, but I immediately recognized her voice. *Ms. Vorax.* "I invited it in, I let the Wendigo take me over. I ate my best friend so I could live. We should've both died. I can't stop, so hungry, so hungry-" She looked into my eyes as she spoke. She seemed scared, revolted, and finally just crazed. Like she would still be trying to eat Mr. Gundy if she could move. I stepped forward and picked her up by her torn throat, my jaws locked around her thin neck. I hesitated. *I knew this woman. How could I just end her life?*

"Finish it! Please! Have mercy on me, God please forgive me. Now, finish me now-" She said in a choked voice. Her eyes glowed red and her face started to change, back to the creature that had taken control of her. Back to the *demon* that had caused her to kill and eat her own best friend, a young boy in a park, an old man who ran a store in town, Arnel, the senior from my school. A beast that had attacked Mr. Gundy *and* Ronan. That would have *eaten* them both. Fear and rage battled inside me. I would weep for Ms. Vorax, but not for this thing. There was no cure for her, the demon had ravaged her very soul. She was dying already, had been since that day in the woods with her friend. I could smell fear and death emanating from her body. She started to twist and elongate, her arm raised, no longer human but some hideous in-between thing, gray skinned with clawed hands. She tried to rake her claws against me. I moved quickly. *Snap!* I felt her throat crush under my powerful jaws. The putrescent blood of the Wendigo filled my mouth. I relaxed my jaws and she fell to the blood-stained floor. A pitiful moan escaped her human again lips, but I saw something more in her eyes before they went permanently vacant. *Peace*, I think.

I walked on four legs over to where Ronan was crouched next to Mr. Gundy. He looked at me with wide green eyes surrounded by thick, copper eyelashes. He stared at me directly for a full-on minute before he cocked his head and looked down. Like he remembered he had to show me he was submissive. He reached a handout and touched my forepaw.

"Hurry, Maria. They'll be here in a minute." I nuzzled his cheek and licked the scratch the Wendigo had given him. I bent my head and tended the wounds on his chest as well. It had angered and scared me to see his blood spilled. He froze in place then ever so carefully, he stroked my head twice. His expression was pained. *Had I offended him?* I was embarrassed by my behavior. *Maybe Werewolves didn't lick people or something? I didn't know. Too late now, anyway.*

Ronan stood up and grabbed my dress and shoes as I ducked behind a bookshelf. It took five minutes this time for me to change back. Ronan must have thrown my dress over the side while I was changing and I quickly put it on despite my sensitized skin. Maybe it was the adrenaline, but it didn't hurt as much as before. He handed me my shoes and as I bent to put them on I noticed as he tucked scraps of what were my underthings in his jacket pocket. Wind was blowing in from a broken window and I realized he must have done that sometime during my change. It felt cool, but still my cheeks burned. *Sure, I was a Werewolf and I had just killed my teacher who happened to be a people eating monster but show a boy my panties and I blushed like crazy! Go figure!*

Ronan looked around at the bodies on the floor. I could hear Mr. Gundy's heartbeat in the silence and was relieved. He was still alive. He'd probably lose his leg, it was gnawed to bits, but he would *live*. And that meant everything. Ronan busied himself wrapping his belt around Mr. Gundy's thigh just above where the wounds were located. Then he grabbed a nearby curtain and tore it from the rings. He wound it around the bite marks that were still bleeding.

Ms. Vorax would not be so lucky. I had snapped her neck in my Wolf jaws. Her limp form on the floor as if she had fallen asleep there. No hint of beast remained. Suddenly I worried about evidence, like my DNA, skin fragments, hair follicles? *OMG!* Would I be arrested? Would everyone find out about me? Panicked my eyes met Ronan's as he worked quickly and with some competence.

"They'll be able to tell it was me! My DNA is everywhere and so is yours! What do we do?"

"Don' worry, your uncle will handle all that."

"How do you know?"

"We take care of our own. He just needs to perform the ritual and all our involvement will be masked. Fancy that, you know, I read about the Wendigo in books about Native American lore, but I never thought they were real." He finished bandaging Mr. Gundy and walked over to Ms. Vorax. He turned her onto her stomach. On her back was a symbol, like a brand. It looked tribal, like a pentagram spiraling out bigger and bigger until it was about palm sized. There were five circles where fingers would be if it were a left hand.

"That's the mark of the demon's masters, the *handprint of the Devil* so to speak. This thing, this Wendigo, was set upon this woman in her moment of weakness and pain. That's the work of witches, it took a lot of blood magic raising this demon. I can still smell the foulness of rot and demon stink on her." Ronan jerked his head back from the scent. His words were laced with venom and his eyes glowed.

"That mark there is the symbol of the coven that let the Wendigo demon out. It must have attached itself to her from the top of her spine. She never stood a chance." He crossed himself and rolled her onto her back once more.

"*Pater Noster, qui es in caelis, sanctificetur nomen tuum...*" He spoke quietly and with reverence and I listened as he finished the Lord's Prayer in Latin. We both looked up, our senses on alert. I heard the sound of someone running down the hallway on light feet in our direction.

"I made a phone call," he said and cleared his throat. He then took my hand and stepped back from the bodies.

Uncle Sean stepped into the room, he seemed on high alert and anxious. He took in the scene with one glance and came to me immediately. "Are you hurt?" he ran his hands along my arms and face and looked me up and down.

"I'm fine, Uncle Sean, Ronan was injured though."

"I don't see anything. Ronan are you okay? Mr. Gundy's alive, I see, good work there, lad." I looked at Ronan and he shook his head slightly. I remembered the way I had licked him and noticed the scratches and gashes were healed. Clearly, he didn't want me to say anything, but I didn't know why.

"No, that wasn't my blood, I'm fine. Mr. Gundy will be fine. I've been listening to his breathing and heart rate."

"So, what happened here then? How did you kill it?" He looked at Ronan.

"*She changed*, Sean, tea and all, your niece changed and *she* killed it."

"That's impossible."

"Nevertheless, it happened." Ronan stood there, tall and proud. His body language letting my uncle know he would stand up for me and protect me no matter what. I was confused and a little frightened, maybe it was the shock of what I had done. Ronan's strength and unwavering faith comforted me.

"Alright. We'll discuss it later. There are bigger

things we need to worry about. They'll be coming now." He walked over to the crime scene and started chanting something in Latin. *I really needed to brush up on my Latin.* After a few seconds, a blue light seemed to shine right from his raised hand. It was bright and ethereal and it engulfed the entire scene. I figured that was what Ronan meant when he said my uncle would "handle it". It lasted barely long enough for me to take my next breath.

"Okay lad, hand me that phone so I can remove evidence of you, right. Now get her out of here." Ronan nodded and tugged my arm, I wanted to stay and argue that we should be there to talk to the police, but by the time I found my voice Ronan had walked us to the broken window and was lifting me through it. I followed him into the woods and we waited as seconds later Sr. Diane, an EMT and a couple of uniformed police officers came barreling into the library. Our Werewolf senses allowed us to see and hear everything that went on. Uncle Sean explained he had seen something going on from the Rectory and went to check it out. When he found the bodies, he dialed 911 and then called Sr. Diane.

"Oh, my goodness, Father Gallagher, was it a bear?"

"Could have been, Sister, by the time I got here it was long gone."

"Okay, sir, ma'am, we'll need to take statements from you both." The female police officer took down their information and radioed in for animal control.

We watched as the EMTs put Mr. Gundy on a gurney and hooked him up to an IV. They didn't bother with Ms. Vorax, clearly, she was dead. Her body was left where it was as crime scene investigators snapped photos and began collecting evidence. Sr. Diane was on the phone, alerting faculty members to go on with the dance.

"No, no, don't tell the students anything. We will deal with it on Monday. Yeah, don't worry, the police are going to place two patrol cars by the gym doors, like an escort. No, they said it's unlikely the bear would return-" She continued like that while Uncle Sean gave his statement to the policewoman. I felt I should say something, anything to Ronan. He beat me to it.

"Hey, you've got a smudge on your cheek." I lifted my hand to wipe my face and collided with his. I dropped mine and allowed him to clear the dirt smudge from my face. His hands were callused, but warm and very gentle. I shivered.

"You're cold. Let's get back, they'll be missing us." His voice sounded rough. I felt my chest tighten. *Sebas-*

tian. How could I have forgotten him? And how could I go back to dancing now? I felt lightheaded. I leaned on Ronan a second and he looked alarmed.

"Are you alright? It's just the change. It was quick this time."

"Yeah, I'm fine."

"Come on." Ronan brought me around to the gym. Sebastian was outside.

"Grazi! Where did you go? I was worried." He jogged over to us and took my hand. I noticed Ronan had immediately dropped my arm when he came into view.

"I, um, I-"

"Your girlfriend here got sick, must've been the fog machine. You should watch out for her better there, *boyo*," Ronan stood taller than Sebastian and he was using his height to intimidate the other boy.

"Yeah, I'll do that," He took a step closer to Ronan. That was *so* not a good idea. I could feel the tension in Ronan. Maybe it was an overload of testosterone from the fight, or the fact that the full moon was so near or maybe it was just a guy thing.

"Hey Sebby, I'm sorry I worried you. You were helping with the decorations and I came outside. Ronan here just stayed with me while I cleared my head."

"Oh, okay. Are you alright?" Sebastian's focus was on me now, not Ronan. *Good.*

"I'm really not feeling very well. The, uh, fog machine made me lightheaded. I'm sorry, but I think I should go home." It was sort of true. I mean, up to that point I must have been running on adrenaline. I felt really drained all of a sudden. I mean, I had just battled for my life a few minutes ago. That was a pretty good reason for leaving the first dance I was ever invited to and oh yeah, *I had no underwear on!*

"Come here, Grazi, sit down on the bench here. Look, I'll go get our coats and call my Dad, alright?" He took off his jacket and draped it over my shoulders, it smelled like him. He hesitated like he didn't want to leave me alone. If he only knew how safe I was.

"No worries, I'll sit with her till you get back." Sebastian hesitated even more after Ronan made that announcement. I just nodded for him to go ahead.

"So, what now?" I looked down at my shoes as I spoke. They were so shiny, so new, untouched by the blood and violence I had just participated in. *Great, now I was getting morbid.*

"What do you mean, princess? You vanquished the demon, saved Mr. Gundy *and* myself, I'd call it a night if I were you. Unless you want to go look for vampires or goblins to battle."

"Very funny. Anyway, what I meant was I guess they're all real. *Demons and stuff.*"

"Yeah, I guess so."

"And I'm real too. I mean I am really what *I am*. We're both, *you know*."

"Yeah, that too."

"Hey, wait a second! Did you just say *vampires* are real too? Like in that movie?"

"Yes, but they don't sparkle and they aren't very attractive."

"Oh, so they're not the mysterious and gorgeous types then?"

"No not really, more like wrinkled bats with huge teeth and bad diets. Now Werewolves are more the mysterious and gorgeous types. Just look for yourself!" We both laughed as he smiled and wagged his eyebrows. I ducked my head. I wasn't sure how I was supposed to feel. Was it okay to be happy? I had just killed someone.

"Look, Maria, you can't think of her as a person. She wasn't human anymore. Her soul and humanity were dead the minute she invited that thing inside her. Understand?"

"I guess so. She probably started stalking her victims away from here, like that boy up in Dover.

Then she must have gotten tired of that and hunted on campus. What do you think?"

"Perhaps. I nicked her phone, figured I'd look some stuff up. The pack will want to figure all that out. The police will think she and Mr. Gundy were attacked by the same rabid animal that's been attacking people." Our conversation paused here and I found the courage to ask him what I really wanted to know.

"Ronan, what I *did* to you. To your wounds. What was that?" Too late I could hear the gym doors creaking open. Sebastian was coming back.

"Another time, princess, ask me another time." Faster than a human eye could see Ronan lifted a lock of hair that had fallen across my face and tucked it behind my ear. His pinky traced a line down my cheek and sent shivers down my spine. I looked away from him, unsure of myself and my reactions. He walked back to the gym. I listened to his footsteps and jumped a little when Sebastian sat down next to me and put his hand on my back.

"Here I brought you a bottle of water." He handed me a mini bottle of spring water. I drank it in one gulp. The taste of Wendigo blood still in the back of my throat, I wanted to vomit but figured I wouldn't push this disaster of a date any further with that kind of display.

"Wow, um, feel any better?" I shook my head. Sebastian was so sweet and understanding. I gave him back his suit jacket and we both put on our coats. He sat next to me and talked to me about all sorts of normal things. I wanted so much right then to be a *normal* girl. It was unfair to make him leave the dance, unfair to drag him into my mess of a life. I'd have to find a way to back out of our tentative relationship. The realization hurt. I held his hand and he smiled. He leaned in and kissed my lips just as a horn blared.

10

I had thought I would have the rest of the night alone in my room to think things through, but when Sebastian's dad dropped me off and peeled off down the street, I noticed a strange car parked in my neighbor's usually empty driveway. It was a large black SUV with tinted windows. No license plates. *Weird*.

I knew Julianna was still at the dance and I could hear Uncle Vito and Aunt Theresa upstairs arguing in their bedroom when I opened the door. Rebecca was most likely asleep, online, or watching television. I walked through the dark living room and decided to go straight to my own without looking for Nonna. I didn't want her to see me like this, it would worry her.

"Maria, *vieni qua,*" I heard her voice from the kitchen "There is someone here to see you." I walked into the lit kitchen. The brightness was harsh to my night vision adjusted eyes. Her stiff posture told me something was wrong. She held her rosary beads tightly in her hand and mumbled under her breath in a mixture of Latin and Italian. *Was she praying?* The smell of freshly brewed tea greeted me as I passed through the oak door frame. Bunches of herbs hung on drying racks along one wall and permeated the air with their powerful fragrances. The kitchen was as warm and friendly as ever. It seemed to invite me in and beg me to taste the succulent wonders hidden behind pantry doors and double refrigerators. But something, or rather, *someone* was out of place.

Sitting in a chair at our kitchen table was an older man. He was *familiar*, but I didn't know him. He had a short mustache and beard that were light brown with steel gray streaks. His hair was the same color and thick and wavy. He was very handsome for an older man and equally formidable. He didn't smile, heck, he hardly blinked. He simply looked me over from head to toe. Like he was judging me. Right then I wasn't too concerned with how I measured up. Instinctively I felt I should fear him, but I didn't for whatever reason.

Maybe it was because I recognized his piercing blue eyes where I couldn't place his face or form. Or maybe it was because I had killed someone that night. *No, Grazi, not someone. You killed a demon.* Whatever the reason, I stared him in the eye until I could feel both his anger and his amusement. I'm not sure who blinked first. He chuckled deep in his throat and took a sip of his steaming tea.

"Well, *garinion*, you're as feisty as your da ever was." He stood smoothly, his large frame taking up most of the space in the kitchen. "Aye, you'll do." He strolled purposely out of the back door without another word or backward glance. His scent stayed behind. I breathed deep as Nonna collapsed into a chair and held her hands over her face. I smelled *Wolf* on him. Powerful and old.

"Nonna, who was that man?"

"Oh, Maria! It is time, the prophecy is happening now and that man, that man, -" She wrung her hands and attempted to compose herself. "That man is the Alpha of Greyback Pack, leader of the Hounds of God. He is your grandfather, Maria. *Signore* Rolf Kelly." Somehow the news didn't shock me. Those familiar eyes of his, I'd seen them a thousand times before. They stared back at me from the pictures in the scrapbooks and photo albums I had stacked in my room. Of course, they were younger there and more carefree. They were my father's eyes.

Well, this was certainly the year for family reunions. I don't know why, but I didn't trust him. How could I? A grandfather who had no interest in me until now? Who killed his own son, *my father*? I didn't think I was capable of dealing with anything else that night. Nonna didn't seem to see me, so I left her alone in the kitchen. I was exhausted and confused, but I felt so dirty. Up in my room I took off my gold lace dress. Miraculously, it had survived the night. I stood under the hot spray of the shower and scrubbed my body furiously with my rubber duck shaped loofah and a bar of Ivory soap. I had to get the stink of rot and death off of me. I had to brush my teeth four times before I was satisfied I was clean and still the memory of Ms. Vorax's face stayed fresh in my mind. Despite Ronan's reassurance, I still wondered if there was something else I could have done. You know, *besides* kill her. I stepped out of the foggy bathroom in my robe and was not surprised to see my uncle sitting by the window. My Wolf had sensed him immediately. He was facing the almost full moon, when he turned towards me I could see his scruffy beard had gotten longer and his eyes were different. More Wolf-like than human.

"You had a busy night, *inion dearthar*."

"Did you know he was coming here?" I stood on the opposite side of the room and waited for his answer.

"How did you do it? How did you change?" His voice was a whisper, but I heard him clearly as if he'd been shouting.

"Did you *know* he was coming?" I repeated, my volume increased with emotion.

"Aye, of course, I did. But too soon, Grazi, he's here too soon. Now please, how did you do it? You drank the tea, the moon, she's not yet full, how could you change? It's impossible!"

"I don't know. I just did."

"He'll oversee your training now, you know. We've little time left."

"What's the prophecy, uncle? Why is he here now?"

"A Wolf unlike any other will lead us to battle for the right to hold dominion over the Earth. It wasn't Patrick at all! It's *you*!"

"You thought it was my father before, didn't you?" Uncle Sean rubbed the top of his head the way he did when deep in thought, but this seemed to be born of anxiety rather than contemplation.

"You followed my father here too, didn't you? Like

Ronan's dad. You knew my mom! You saw her die!" My accusation hung between us in the room. My uncle's shoulders sagged in defeat.

"I'd never have had her hurt for anything, Grazi. Lilliana was supposed to be home that night! She was, she was ill and she, just- She was supposed to be home! I was supposed to stay with her! But Patrick, I wanted to help Patrick, my big brother." My uncle's shoulders shook as tears rolled unabashedly down his face. I heard my Wolf howl in my mind. I didn't move, didn't want to comfort him. I don't know, maybe I was a bit harsh, but there was still so much I didn't understand. And he was holding back. That's the thing about Werewolves, we can actually *smell* a lie. Even one of omission.

"Someone let the Wendigo out, Uncle Sean, who?"

"I don't know. I'm sorry, Grazi. And you're right, I failed her. *Oh God, Lilly*. But I won't fail you. That's my vow, daughter of my brother, I'll not rest until I've found out who is responsible." He left shortly after. There was nothing more to say.

I sat at the window and looked out at the remnants of our garden. What a terrible season we had had! This cold front was not helping any either. What was going on with the weather? Months of heat and drought followed by bitter cold. It was awful. Suddenly lightning flashed in the sky, followed by loud thunder. Miracle of miracles, rain started to fall. A light splattering at first, but *so* needed. I could practically hear the plants rejoice. I opened my window and climbed out onto the sill. I breathed in the fresh scent of the rain and let it soak through my robe. The cold drops ran down my face and body, I tilted my head back and relished in it. It was such a wonderful relief from the putrid stink of death and fear and blood.

So, there was a prophecy about a Wolf who would lead the Hounds to glory in some big battle. And all in the name of God. And that Wolf was supposed to be *me*. I didn't know what to make of it. I mean I was still just a girl, wasn't I? I tried to push those thoughts out of my head and enjoy the rainfall. *Clear your mind, little one. You have won tonight. We will face tomorrow together.*

I jumped back inside my room and pulled a crocheted blanket Nonna had made for me out of the window seat. I dropped my wet robe and wrapped the warm fuzzy blanket around me. I knelt back down on the cushioned seat. I knew I had to get ready for bed, but not just yet. I closed the glass window and surveyed the garden and the woods beyond trying to make sense out of the fantastic events that had occurred. That's when I saw a pair of glowing eyes watching me from behind the tall pine trees beyond the back fence of our yard. My Wolf snarled in alarm. I stood and tried to get a closer look, but they were gone with the next flash of lightning. Maybe I imagined it? I stood and closed the curtains. Plenty of time to think about it tomorrow. I fell asleep fitfully and dreamt of my mother.

From that night on Nonna's attitude changed. She no longer wept for me but seemed to accept my place in things. Something of a feat since *I* didn't accept my place yet. She started putting little statues of the saints, Jesus, and Mary all over my room. Even taking down some of my rubber ducks to place them on my shelves. My appetite was growing, and she always made sure we had fresh organic roasted turkey breasts and whole baked fish on hand all the time. She wouldn't invite my grandfather or uncle or even Ronan over for dinner, not even on a Sunday, but I guess I couldn't blame her.

Nonna calls me a *benendanta,* something out of Italian folklore. Uncle Sean calls me a *Hound of God.* Ronan simply uses *Werewolf* or, when he is feeling playful, *Wolfgirl2014.* Well, whatever I am, I am still *me.* I am still a teenage girl with all the same drama as anyone else. I still had midterms, PMS, college brochures, mean girls to deal with, and a crush on the cutest boy in school. I just also had to worry about an upcoming supernatural battle with witches in order to save the world. *No biggie.*

A NOTE FOR MY AMAZING READERS:

Hello!

Thank you so much for reading Wolf Moon! This is the first book in my YA Urban Fantasy Series. These are clean reads appropriate for any age.

The Grazi Kelly Universe is growing by leaps and bounds and I have plans to increase it even further! Please be advised my Paranormal Romance Books are recommended for mature audiences and contain adult content.

If you read PNR, be sure to check out how the Macconwood Pack all started with *Wolf Bride* and *Charley's Christmas Wolf*. I've got Werewolves, Dhampirs, Bears, and Dragons in or near my fictional town of Maccon City! And did you know the Pine Barrens are home to one hell of a Devil? Find these and more on my website.

It's back to my writing cave for now!

del mare alla stella,

C.D. Gorri

**Before you go any further, sign up for my newsletter and get the latest on my releases, giveaways, freebies and more:*

C.D. Gorri's Newsletter Link!

P.S

Hello Awesome Reader!

Don't forget to tell me how you liked this story by leaving your honest review!

No pressure. 😊

A review can be one or two brief sentences where you simply state whether you enjoyed the story and would recommend it to someone! It is an enormous help to authors and the best way for us to reach larger audiences so we can keep writing the stories you love!

Thank you so much!

Xoxo!
Del mare alla stella,
C.D. Gorri

P.S.

Don't forget to sign up for my newsletter!
www.cdgorri.com/newsletter

LOOK FOR MORE YA/URBAN FANTASY FROM C.D. GORRI

Welcome to my Young Adult Urban Fantasy Books!

Including:
The Grazi Kelly Novel Series
The Angela Tanner Files
G'Witches Magical Mysteries Series

& New Adult Urban Fantasy
The Witches of Westwood Academy
Blackthorn Academy for Supernaturals

To me, the world of the paranormal is full of endless possibilities. As a writer, I can take advantage of that. I can introduce old ideas through new characters and situations. And hopefully, I can entertain you while trying to do just that.

All of my books are set in the same paranormal world and mainly take place in my home state of New Jersey. I call it the Grazi Kelly Universe in honor of my first heroine, Maria Graziana Kelly aka Grazi (grah-tzee). Characters and creatures overlap, but each series can be read alone.

So far, I've expanded this world to encompass Werewolves or Wolf Shifters, Witches, Demons, Dragon Shifters, Bear Shifters, Fox Shifters, Jaguar Shifters, and more! It is my intention to continue to build this world with every book I write.

These books are clean reads unless otherwise stated. Some are part of a series, others are standalone.

Del mare alla stella,
C.D. Gorri

EXCERPT FROM HUNTER MOON

Chapter 1

Tearing through the bitter cold in the dead of night should have been scary. The frigid air made streaming clouds of my breath as I ran through the woods. An enormous black Wolf to the left of me pulled his mouth back, revealing long sharp canines. He howled and plunged ahead. A few inches to his right and he could have easily taken me down. Of that I have no doubt. I wasn't afraid though. I was exhilarated.

The full moon shone down through the trees. It threw shadows off the tall pines, birches and oaks. We ran for about fifteen or twenty miles. It was difficult for me to tell as I hurried to keep up with the rest of the pack. The scenery sped wildly by, but I was much too aware of everything not to notice. I flew past towering walnut trees and bare forsythias. My large forepaws pounded the earth as I launched myself over fallen branches and dried out shrubs.

The smell of the woods mixed with that of my companions filled my sensitive nostrils. I could make out each distinct member of our party by scent alone. I listened and was deafened by the beating of our hearts, our breathing, the scurrying of small forest animals avoiding us, and the hoot of an owl as it clung to a tall tree overhead. *Overwhelming?* Maybe at another time I would have felt that way. But this was different.

It wasn't exactly as if time had slowed down. It was more like I was *in* every moment. Something I had never experienced before. I had no idea where we were going. I blindly followed the pack. Too focused on everything and everyone around me to be worried about something as ordinary as our destination.

My gaze landed on Ronan. He was ahead of me by a body length. I could make out every single strand of his red and gold fur. It made his coat glow like fire when the moonlight hit it. He moved on four legs with the same beautiful grace that he did on two. I often found myself watching him at school or when we jogged together. He was fast and agile. But more than that. He was *elegant* for someone so tall and muscular.

I wondered if I moved like that too. Was I graceful and competent? I didn't used to be. But everything was different now. He turned his long lupine head toward me. His green eyes burning in the darkness. I snorted at him and he yipped. He was checking on me as he had done several times. I didn't resent it as much as I pretended too.

It was the first time I'd run as a Wolf in the company of others. In fact I'd never seen a pack before. Even a small pack as this one was. I had googled Wolves in my spare time and knew I was much larger than a wild grey Wolf. Seeing the others before me made me realize I was, if anything, average sized for my kind. My fur was a dark brownish color and I had a platinum streak running down my muzzle. It matched the one in my hair that I got after my first change. I'm almost used to it. Well, at least I don't jump every time I see my reflection anymore.

I already knew what my Wolf looked like. I've seen her in my mind's eye, when she spoke to me. I knew the form I took now from my pointed ears right down to the tip of my furry tail. I was stronger, faster, and a lot more lethal like this. I think I might even weigh more as a Wolf than I do as a girl. My appetite certainly has increased. I'm thinking it must have more to do with my Wolf side since I haven't gained all that much weight. The pounds I've put on seem to be mostly muscle anyway. I am totally good with that since I looked a little like a string bean before.

The full moon hung low in the sky. Huge and golden it touched me with its light. I felt whole and strong with power. The air was thick with it. I used to always think of darkness when I thought of the night. But not now. *The true light of the moon and the stars is always present, but we can only see it in the darkest night.* That's something my Uncle Sean told me. He was right. It was incredible. Especially through these eyes.

Uncle Sean's huge shaggy blonde Wolf ran directly behind his father, Rolf. He was larger than the all of the rest of us except for my grandfather. He was a massive white Wolf with steel gray eyes and an unmistakable air of dominance. He led the hunt. Uncle Sean had advised me before we changed that this is the way it was done. Werewolves are pretty serious about their pecking order. Alpha's tended to get snooty if anyone ran in front of them. It was in their nature to be first, to guard the pack from whatever may lie ahead.

I ran somewhere near the back of our party. I wondered what that meant for me in the greater scheme of things. Guess I'm pretty low on the dominance list. That's just fine with me. The other Werewolves spent a few minutes snapping and growling before order was established and Rolf commanded we move. Ronan stayed near me and kept tabs throughout our run. There were four large Werewolves that flanked us on all sides. One was the black Wolf who liked to show off his fangs, two more were gray and another was a honey color. Guards, all of them. I didn't know their names. They hadn't been introduced to me when we met at my grandfather's new home base, which incidentally happened to be next door to my house.

Maybe I should back up a step. My name is Maria Graziana Kelly, most people call me Grazi (*grah-tzee*). A few months ago, I found out that I'm a real live Werewolf. Yup, that's right, I tend to get furry around the full moon. I'm also bound by an ancient pact my ancestors made to serve with the Hounds of God. They're like this mega Wolf pack who technically work for the Catholic Church. The Hounds have been fighting an age old battle against covens of Witches who want to claim dominion over the Earth for the Devil. You heard me correctly, I seriously mean the actual *Devil*.

My father before me was a Hound. He and my mother died fighting this battle when I was about three years old. I keep a picture of them next to my bed. I was raised by my maternal grandmother, Nonna Rosa.

Hard to believe? *You betcha.* I didn't really buy it either until last night when I got all furry and fangy and ripped the throat out of my high school librarian.

Of course, I only did that after she turned out to be possessed by a Wendigo. A ravenous Demon who was responsible for several local deaths including a student at my high school, Sacred Heart Prep. Wendigos eat their victims. They crave human flesh. The more they consume, the deeper the craving. Scary, right? But they aren't the only things out there. This world is new to me, but I have to survive it. *I just have to.* To find out what really happened to my parents. And to avenge them.

The eight of us came to a clearing in the woods. Ronan stayed by my side and I waited as Rolf continued in the lead. I had no problem keeping to the rear. It was his right to lead. He was, after all, the Alpha. He stealthily crouched down. Everyone stopped and mimicked him. I did too. I could smell the small creatures we were stalking and my mouth filled with saliva. *Ew.*

Ronan had told me before we changed that we were going hunting. *Rabbits.* Six of them were tucked into a hole beneath the cold, dried up grass. I could hear their tiny hearts racing and it made me salivate more. *Yuck.* I'd never eaten rabbit, but the beast in me could have devoured the lot whole. I shuddered. *I am so not normal.* I shook my head which earned me a stern look from Mr. I-like-to-show-off-my fangs.

Rolf signaled with a swish of his tail for the guards to come in closer. Another swish, the lowering of his ears, and the hunt began. Rabbits darted in all directions, sensing our presence, and we chased them. I watched Uncle Sean shake his prize in his jaws until the tiny creature's neck snapped. He was busy digging in when I felt something strange. I let the small brown bunny I was stalking go and picked my head up. It was like something was watching me. Stalking *me*, the hunter. I didn't like it.

While the other Wolves took advantage of the power bestowed on us by the full moon, I watched the woods.

Our four guards were no longer *guarding* us. They were caught up in the thrill and satisfaction of the hunt. Ronan, Uncle Sean, and Rolf seemed intent on the game also. *Not Me.* No, I felt *exposed*. Threatened. Something was definitely not right.

I scanned the tree line for something, anything that could explain what I was feeling. Rolf yipped at me. I made a move to join him, but stopped mid-step. Were-Wolves can communicate, but it wasn't like the way I had talked to Ronan before. It was more like images and impressions. I could tell he was not pleased by my behavior.

I felt Rolf trying to pressure me. To bend me to his will. *Hunt. Eat. Obey.* I wanted too, I really did, but I forced myself to step back. Away from him and his commands. Not without struggle, mind you. But I managed it.

He bared his fangs, flattened his ears, and loosed a short growl. *No.* I would not challenge him. I dropped my eyes and took another backwards step. He turned his back on me then. His attention back on his prey. A large brown rabbit. *Yum.* My Wolf wanted some of the succulent, juicy meat, but *I* was in control.

I sniffed the air. I smelled Wolf, rabbit blood, the cold forest, and something else. Something a little off. Waves of color surrounded the Wolves. Mostly the same reds, oranges. They were stronger around Rolf and Sean. My Wolf eyes watched the colors for a moment.

I didn't know what they meant. I looked at the trees and they too had their own colors, greens and golds. It was strange and beautiful. Another advantage of my Wolf's eyes perhaps? I could only assume so.

I walked slowly in a circle surrounding the others. The feeling was back. Someone or something was out there. I continued to look among the bare branches and frost covered bark of the surrounding trees. My body stopped moving the second I saw them. A pair of glowing eyes. The same set I thought I had imagined just last night from my bedroom window.

They held mine for a moment before disappearing. I took off at full speed heading for what, I did not know. Only Ronan seemed to notice. He yipped and followed me. I could feel his disapproval. He wanted to stay and enjoy his prize. His Wolf belly grumbled loudly. Hungry again, for sure. I loosed a short howl and charged ahead confident he'd follow. I was glad to have him. I mean even after everything I had seen, who knew what waited for me in the darkness?

I stopped short in a small clearing. Ronan skidded to a stop directly behind me.

Someone's here, Ronan.

What? Where?

Wait, is that you? Can you hear me like this too? It was like an open line of communication between my mind and Ronan's had opened up. His thoughts voiced clearly in my mind and his impressions too. The foremost one was his desire to protect me. Always.

Yeah, Maria, I think I can. This is crazy. We should get back to the others.

Why? They won't listen. Rolf won't listen.

Where are we going then?

I sniffed the air. I smelled forest, the cold, a faint whiff of a bear that must have passed within the last day or so, and Ronan, his Wolf musk pleasant to my sensitive nose. There was something else. It was mineral like. Iron or copper. Nope. I knew what it was.

Do you smell that, Ronan? It's blood.

Yes, I smell it. Let's get back. Rolf is angry and he's calling us, can you not feel him?

I can, but it's faint. I can shake it off.

What do you mean shake it off? It's deafening.

No, it's more like a whisper now that we aren't near him.

What are you, Maria Graziana?

I don't understand.

I know you don't. Let's go. We will report what we have found...

OTHER TITLES BY C.D. GORRI

Other Titles by C.D. Gorri

Young Adult Urban Fantasy Books:

Wolf Moon: A Grazi Kelly Novel Book 1

Hunter Moon: A Grazi Kelly Novel Book 2

Rebel Moon: A Grazi Kelly Novel Book 3

Winter Moon: A Grazi Kelly Novel Book 4

Chasing The Moon: A Grazi Kelly Short 5

Blood Moon: A Grazi Kelly Novel 6

*Get all 6 books NOW AVAILABLE IN A BOXED SET:

The Complete Grazi Kelly Novel Series

Casting Magic: The Angela Tanner Files 1

Keeping Magic: The Angela Tanner Files 2

G'Witches Magical Mysteries Series

Co-written with P. Mattern

G'Witches

G'Witches 2: The Hary Harbinger

Home for the Howlidays: A Macconwood Pack Tale 6

A Silver Wedding: A Macconwood Pack Tale 7

Mine Furever: A Macconwood Pack Tale 8

A Furry Little Christmas: A Macconwood Pack Tale 9

Also available in two boxed sets:

The Macconwood Pack Tales Volume 1

Shifters Furever: The Macconwood Pack Tales Volume 2

The Falk Clan Tales:

The Dragon's Valentine: A Falk Clan Novel 1

The Dragon's Christmas Gift: A Falk Clan Novel 2

The Dragon's Heart: A Falk Clan Novel 3

The Dragon's Secret: A Falk Clan Novel 4

The Dragon's Treasure: A Falk Clan Novel 5

Dragon Mates: The Falk Clan Series Boxed Set Books 1-4

The Bear Claw Tales:

Bearly Breathing: A Bear Claw Tale 1

Bearly There: A Bear Claw Tale 2

Bearly Tamed: A Bear Claw Tale 3

Bearly Mated: A Bear Claw Tale 4

Also available in a boxed set:

The Complete Bear Claw Tales (Books 1-4)

The Barvale Clan Tales:

Polar Opposites: The Barvale Clan Tales 1

Polar Outbreak: The Barvale Clan Tales 2

Polar Compound: A Barvale Clan Tale 3

Polar Curve: A Barvale Clan Tale 4

Also available in a boxed set:

The Barvale Clan Tales (Books 1-4)

Barvale Holiday Tales:

A Bear For Christmas

Hers To Bear

Thank You Beary Much

Also available in a boxed set:

The Barvale Holiday Tales (Books 1-3)

Purely Paranormal Romance Books:

Marked by the Devil: Purely Paranormal Romance Books

Mated to the Dragon King: Purely Paranormal Romance Books

Claimed by the Demon: Purely Paranormal Romance Books

Christmas with a Devil, a Dragon King, & a Demon: Purely Paranormal Romance Books

Vampire Lover: Purely Paranormal Romance Books

Grizzly Lover: Purely Paranormal Romance Books

Elvish Lover: Purely Paranormal Romance Books

Hot Dire Wolf Nights: Purely Paranormal Romance Books

Christmas With Her Chupacabra: Purely Paranormal
Romance Books

The Wardens of Terra:

Bound by Air: The Wardens of Terra Book 1

Star Kissed: A Wardens of Terra Short

Waterlocked: The Wardens of Terra Book 2

Moon Kissed: A Wardens of Terra Short

*Now in a boxed set and in audio!

The Maverick Pride Tales:

Purrfectly Mated

Purrfectly Kissed

Purrfectly Trapped

& More coming

Dire Wolf Mates:

SERIES MAKEOVER COMING SOON

Wyvern Protection Unit:

SERIES MAKEOVER COMING SOON

Standalones:

The Enforcer

Blood Song: A Sanguinem Council Book

Sealed Fate

<u>A Howlin' Good Fairytale Retelling</u>

Sweet As Candy (as seen in Once Upon An Ever After)

Shelly Maypo Mysteries

Spring Fling (co-written with P. Mattern)

<u>Coming Soon:</u>

If The Shoe Fits: A Howlin' Good Fairytale Retelling

For Fangs Sake

Moongate Island Captive

The Dragon's Surprise

The Dragon's Dream

Bearing Gifts

Taming Magic: The Angela Tanner Files 3

Vampire Shield: Guardians of Chaos 6

Chickee and the Paparazzi: FUCN'A

The Wolf's Winter Wish: A Macconwood Pack Tale

The Hybrid Assassin

Tiger Rejected

ABOUT THE AUTHOR

C.D. Gorri is a USA Today Bestselling author of steamy paranormal romance and urban fantasy. She is the creator of the Grazi Kelly Universe.

Join her mailing list here: https://www.cdgorri.com/newsletter

An avid reader with a profound love for books and literature, when she is not writing or taking care of her family, she can usually be found with a book or tablet in hand. C.D. lives in her home state of New Jersey where many of her characters or stories are based. Her tales are fast paced yet detailed with satisfying conclusions.

If you enjoy powerful heroines and loyal heroes who face relatable problems in supernatural settings, journey into the Grazi Kelly Universe today. You will find sassy, curvy heroines and sexy, love-driven heroes who find their HEAs between the pages. Werewolves, Bears, Dragons, Tigers, Witches, Romani, Lynxes, Foxes, Thunderbirds, Vampires, and many more Shifters and supernatural creatures dwell within her worlds. The most important thing is every mate in this universe is fated, loyal, and true lovers always get their happily ever afters.

Want to know how it all began? Enter the Grazi Kelly Universe with Wolf Moon: A Grazi Kelly Novel or pick up Charley's Christmas Wolf and dive into the Macconwood Pack Novel Series today.

For a complete list of C.D. Gorri's books visit her website here:

https://www.cdgorri.com/complete-book-list/

Thank you and happy reading!

del mare alla stella,
    C.D. Gorri

Follow C.D. Gorri here:
    http://www.cdgorri.com

https://www.facebook.com/Cdgorribooks

https://www.bookbub.com/authors/c-d-gorri

https://twitter.com/cgor22

https://instagram.com/cdgorri/

https://www.goodreads.com/cdgorri

https://www.tiktok.com/@cdgorriauthor